GIRL IN THE WALLS

KATY MICHELLE QUINN

CLASH

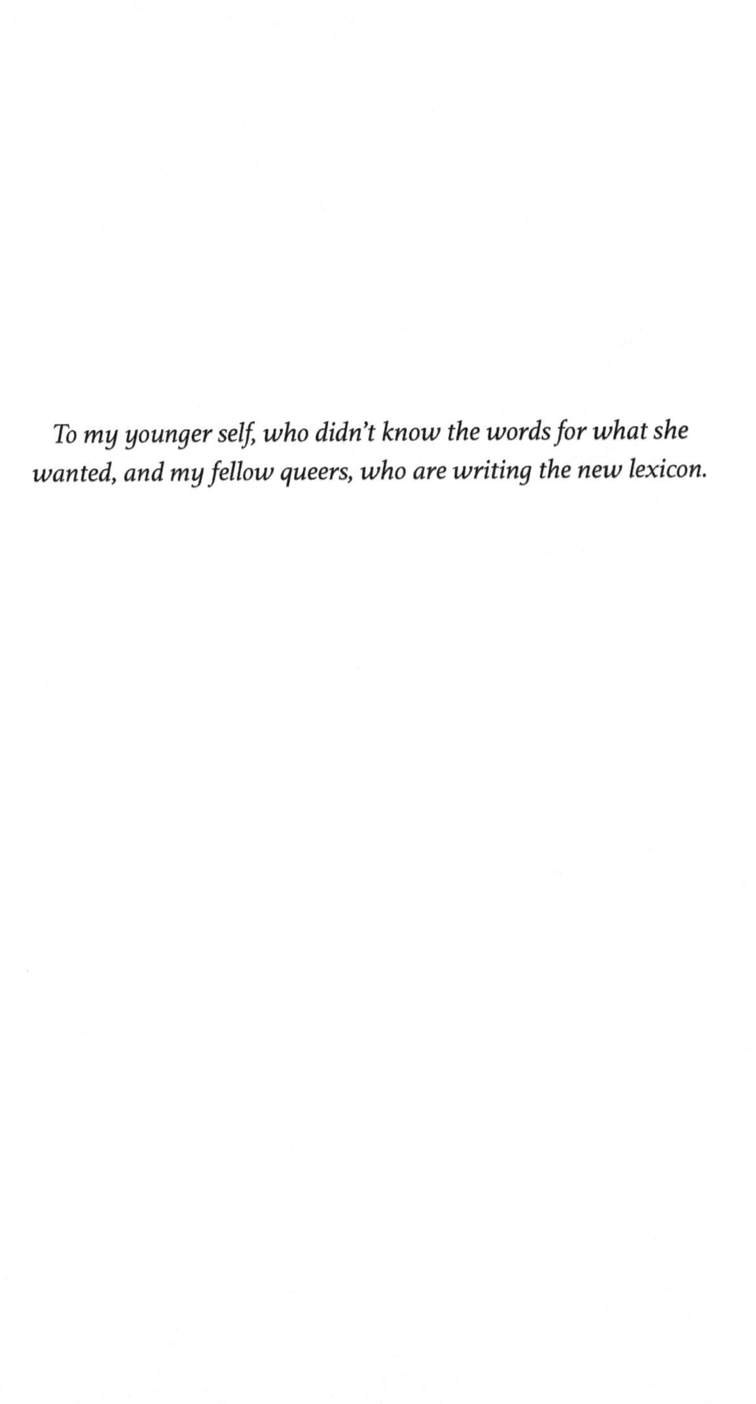

To my younger self, who didn't know the words for what she wanted, and my fellow queers, who are writing the new lexicon.

1

A puddle of purple infects the woodslat flooring of my bedroom, bits of glass glittering within. The same shade stains my fingernails, edges flecked from a bad habit of clawing at my skin. Brawny boys called me a fag, but that was only punctuation on the day, and I've never been a fan of grammar. People, places, and things tell me this isn't the city in bold italics. You can't haunt your way home from school, hiding in plain sight from screen-soaked strangers as they wordlessly press past. Not here. Every flaw is faulted for the ways it doesn't match the mold. The drape of my hair, the color of my nails aren't things that make a man, and you better buck up, Buck-O, cause soon you're gonna be one. My only responses are the marks that darken my arms, a pattern of pain I paint daily.

Dad drew us out here with the promises of cheap living and clean air, code for, a more traditional town. He knew a city secondhand like him would be overvalued by any family company for his skills. Within a month, he found a small-town manufacturer willing to give him a six-figure salary and their firstborn if he would but grace them with his managerial prowess. Of all the things in the world, men make the least sense to me.

So, we packed our minivan and teased the trailing U-Haul two hours toward the Cascades. The safety of the city left behind, and provincial bliss before us in the form of too many churches and a diner named *Bob's Burger Barn*. Two seconds down Main, and I could tell it was the kind of town where everything was as bland, white, and wholesome as milk.

Not that the old school was great, but the new one was even worse. In Seattle, I could sink into my seat and go unnoticed for days. There was enough medley that my long hair and painted nails were hardly a call for insults. There were bullies, sure, but the teachers were woke enough to bring the hammer down hard if someone was teased about how they looked. I was thirteen. Young enough that my experimentation was expected. I mean, who doesn't like purple nails and pink highlights in their hair. It's all fun, right? It'll pass once the hormones kick in.

This place is different. Here, boys wear blue and girls wear pink, and anyone who doesn't better have a damn good reason. My first day in class, I was told to cut my hair if I wanted to be invited back. I hadn't worn polish that day, but I was wise enough to know that would've been strike two. Mom took me to the hairdressers straight after school, told the white-haired man working there to "buzz it." He just chuckled as he revved the rustic clippers and told me to cinch your skirt, Nancy, it's all coming off. As I cried into the carnage, my mother flipped through *People* magazine with a look guilty as a criminal.

That was a week ago, though it feels like it's been months. With my peachfuzz skull bared for the world, I drudge through school days trying to avoid the stares from the farm kids wondering what in tarnation the new kid is. No one has said much to me, but they treat me with all the respect of a stray. Too nice to kick it, too disgusted to acknowledge it's there. Fine with me, as long as they leave me alone. I have no interest in joining the boys' flyers' up circle after class, and I'm not sure the girls would let me gossip with them if I wanted to.

My favorite part of every school day is the sound my shoes make as I sludge my way home in the rain. That, and the old Craftsman we had snagged from someone's dead gran. Something about it beckons me deeper. Standing in the doorway is like lingering at the mouth of a forest cave, sifting through shadows. You can smell magic in the air, but you're afraid of what danger lies in the darkness. The oak floorboards are scuffed with decades of ungainly kitten heels, claw marks left by century-old civility. The walls have soaked in the scent of yesterday, a mixture of cigarettes and incense and water-rot. And you were always met with the tense type of silence you might feel in an abandoned barnhouse. A sense of peace armed with teeth.

A fan of any story involving old wood and ghosts, I loved the feel that these walls contained secret stories that I'd be told if I were lucky.

My bedroom was even better. As soon as I scamper up the stairs, I shut the weathered door behind me and let the click of the lock usher in the quiet. Everything the house emanated, the spook and stench and silence, they were tenfold in here. The walls more watermarked, the boards older and overworn, the quiet corners preparing to pounce.

The dinge of my room, I've decided, is the perfect place to plant myself, and every afternoon after school is when I leave everything outside my room behind. This is my time. I am a forest of one planted in planks of dark oak, and here I flourish.

LIKE ANY DAY, today I had pulled out my secret shoebox from under my bed and bumbled through its bottles to find the color I'll paint my nails today. I always wipe it off before bed, but it's nice to be myself a moment.

Unlike any day, though, today the bottle had slipped from my hand, two nails from completion, and shattered, violet liquid soaking into the woodslat floor. My favorite shade, the one I use most often, now a broken waste. It's not like I can buy more, not around here. It's a tiny enough town that someone would tell someone and before you know, my ass is kicked three ways before lunch.

I cry for longer than even I would care to admit. Times like these, I would hide in my hair, but the stubble on my skull provides no comfort. I lay next to the wreckage of the vial like a dead lover and let myself spill with it. My eyes burn, and my skin itches. There's something inside that needs out, too much sad flooding my veins that I might just burst. I reach for a shard of glass. I've gotten in trouble for this before, but nothing seals the sorrow like a few slices down the skin. I push the broken edge into my dermis and drag, heart speeding as blood seeps out of me.

A sound like tearing paper startles me out of my stupor. I notice a small slash in the old floral wallpaper, but besides that the room is undisturbed. Again, I scrape glass across skin. The sound repeats, louder, and I fall back, watching the tear in the wall witch its way wider.

What the actual fuck.

I stand up to inspect the damage. As I do, my veins leak a few streams that intermix with the polish I spilled. They marble a moment, my blood floating through the puddle like a ghost before dissipating. My attention shifts to the slice in the wall, and I reach out to trace the gap with my finger. The area around the tear feels mucky and insubstantial, as if the space behind is hollow. A cool, dank breeze confirms my theory. I give my arm another exploratory nick, and the wall replicates my wound, the hole tearing wider sympathetically. I plunge the fingers of my well hand into the hole, feeling as far as I can into the space beyond. Inside, the air feels cool and wet like an evening in early autumn. I peel back the paper to look, and my pulse pumps triple-time as I rip my arm from the wall. In the dimness, a pair of pale globes blink and then float deeper into the darkness.

"Hey!" I yell.

The eyes hover and coast to a stop.

"Hello?" someone who is not me says.

It sounds like a girl around my age.

Is she stuck inside the walls?

As far as I know, there is no way in or out.

Without thinking I cut my arm harder, letting the blood fall off my fingers. The tear in the wall doubles, triples, rips wide open. The light illuminates a face, though the girl skitters away as soon as it hits her. I drag the shard across my arm one, two, three, four, five times, and the wall follows my lead. My forearm is more red than flesh, and I feel dizzy, but with a sound like static, the wall opens from my waist to my head and just as wide. I stop cutting and let the glass clink to the floor.

I speak, but the only sound I make is like air escaping a tire as I take in what I see. Inside the wall, looking back at me, is a girl around my age. She blinks in the brightness, though she looks as fresh as if she had just walked in from the street. Not decomposed, not ragged, not dirty in any way. Her pale skin shimmers in the dark of the wallspace, and her dirty blond hair cascades down her shoulders. I feel a pang of envy as I remember how mine did the same not long ago. The girl smiles the kind of careful smile you'd offer someone you're meeting for the first time.

"Hi!" she says.

Then I black out.

2

The first thing I see is the sun. It filters through the evergreens outside, and casts a greenish hue to the fog of questions I awoke with. I'm in bed, sheets pulled up to my chin like it's any morning.

My phone beeps its 7:15 school-day alarm, and I slide the screen to dismiss it.

I must've blacked out hard.

The last thing I remember is the echo of a voice coming from, I'm not sure. It sounded familiar, friendly, but who was it? And the eyes, the bright eyes hanging in the dark like unexplored moons, pulling me in with their gravity. I shake the sleep out of my head. That couldn't have been real. It must've been blood loss, or, I dunno. Anything but fact.

How did I get in bed anyway?

If I was out that long, my parents could've found me. Though if they hadn't, it wouldn't have been the first time they interpreted an unanswered dinner call as adolescent angst.

I sit up and look around the room, shucking myself out of my sheets. The walls are dirty, but intact. No sign of any tearing or damage, just the dingy floral pattern laced over the boards like it grew there. The hole I had seen the night before had closed completely.

Or it was never there.

Swinging my legs over the side of my mattress, I shiver as skin hits cold floor. The sensation shocks me onto my feet, and I stretch a sec before stepping towards the wall to inspect it closer. Instinct causes me to pause just in time to save my foot from broken glass, but when I look down to examine the mess, I find nothing.

The fuck?

The woodslat floor dulls the morning light, no sign of broken glass or spilt polish. Maybe it was Mom. Maybe she found me passed out, put me in bed, and cleaned up the mess. That would be unlike her though. Ever since she walked in on me masturbating with my teddy bear at age 12, she had a rigid rule of knocking before she entered my bedroom. It was as if we had formed an unspoken contract of *don't ask/don't tell,* and she had respected it lest she finds another story to tell her therapist.

Turning back, I clump knees-to-floor and feel for the shoebox under my bed, pulling it out quickly and shedding its cover. The bottles inside are rowed up dark to light, a system of organization I had never subscribed to. I thumb through them and my body shakes as my finger falls on my favorite vial. Violet. The one that had been smashed on my floor the evening before. Pulling it from its home, I watch the liquid slide inside the glass. It's half-full, as it was before it had broken. If my Mom replaced it overnight, which seemed unlikely, she had poured half of it out, which seemed unlikelier. Anyway, my parents aren't fans of my feminine side, and the prospect of me losing polish would hardly have them losing sleep.

"Vernon!" Mom knocks through my door. "Time to go to school!"

Fuck. That answers that.

Her typical morning bugle tells me that to her, there is nothing wrong. She must not know I passed out.

I replace the shoebox lid and push my secret stash of cosmetics back under the bed.

"Coming," I say, with a pointed lack of enthusiasm.

I whip off my pajamas and slip into a tee shirt and a pair of skinny jeans. As I pull on my pants, I notice that eight of my nails are still painted. I half-expected that to be gone too, with the bottle mended and replaced. I thought that I had imagined everything, down to the broken glass, but my eight purple nails tell a different story. As I dress, I notice the trails of red lining my forearm. I run fingertips over the bumps where each cut had scabbed into a crust overnight, picking at them a bit with painted fingers. I cut enough to know what a day-old scab looked like, and these are younger than that.

"Vernon?"

"Yeah!"

I stop picking and button my jeans. As I head towards the door, I sling my backpack over my shoulder and pause. I walk to where the wall had opened the night before, feeling the paper that had torn as I ran the glass across my skin. It feels bumpy, organic. As if it too had healed during the night.

My door slams against its frame as my mother unleashes a final barrage of knocks.

"Vernon, come on!" she yells. "You can't just ignore me!"

A moment passes.

"I'm coming in," she says.

As the knob turns, I pull it open to see my mother's face the same cherry red as her nails.

"Finally!" she says. "You're gonna drive me insane, hiding

in your room like that. Skipping dinner is one thing, but I won't let you skip school."

I respond by walking out of my bedroom and closing the door behind me. My mom jogs down the stairs and, loping, I follow.

❧

WHEN WE PULL up to Maple Middle, the building is already buzzing. Mom eases the car through the lot past rows of dirty farm trucks and beat-up imports, our sparkling minivan shining like a sore star among the trash-on-wheels accumulated in front of the school. As if it wasn't obvious enough I was a city kid. Kids and teens groggily gallop out of passenger-side doors, dilapidated packs strapped to their backs, tight as rifles. Our van squeaks to a stop.

"I'll see you after school," Mom says.

I nod, clenching my fists in a way that hides the purple polish on my fingertips. I can tell that Mom notices, but she looks the other way and waits for me to push open the heavy door and make my exit. It's a small kindness she doesn't always afford me, but I'm grateful for it today.

"Yeah," I say, unsure what I'm responding to.

I slump out the sliding door, face buried in the concrete. I learned long ago that eye contact is a poison. I excel in the art of acting aloof. If you aren't present enough to see the small stares or hear the whispered gossip, it makes it a lot easier to get through the day.

With a crunch, our minivan pulls away cruelly. I eek through the twin blue doors at the front of the school, the roar of rowdy children nearly blowing me off my feet. I pick my path and wade into the riptide that is the middle school hallway. I'm halfway to first period when I hear it, quiet at first, then louder.

"Faggot."

I look up, in the off chance they aren't talking about me. The slur slipped from a beefsteak of a boy, shaved head and XXL sports tee covering the beginnings of a beer belly. He catches me looking at him and takes it as a response. Whether he was talking about me or not, he is now. My fearful gaze is the kindling that starts the fire.

"Hey! Hey!" big boy bellows. "New kid's got polish on his nails! New kid's a faggot! Look at that little fag!"

Puberty has blessed him with a deep voice and above-average height, and he flings the insults to over the heads of the student body like predatory pop-flies. A few of his cronies join in the revelry as I push past the wall of kids forming a fight circle.

"*Fag*-got! *Fag*-got!"

The rest of the watchers do just that, bystanding their way into an early mediocrity. A few girls in black roll their eyes at Beef Boy as he tries to make the chant infect. One of them holds up a finger to him.

"Why don't you shut up, you brainless hick?" she yells. "Polish doesn't mean he's gay!"

He stops shouting, the challenge tackling his wit, or lack thereof.

I throw the group of goths a *thank you* look as I fast-walk to first period, getting as far as I can past the flock of jocks. As I near the door, tears drip from my chin and soak into my tee. I wipe my face dry before shuffling into the classroom and sneaking through empty desks to settle in the back row.

"Great to see you, Mr. Weber."

I recognize the cream-and-coffee tone of Mr. Hofstedter's voice. The close-cropped man scrolls through the screen of the dated computer in the back of the class. In the short time I had attended Maple Middle, Mr. Hofstedter had become the only teacher I attempted to trust. He's a soft-edged sort with a secret, and I feel at least a little understood by him.

"Hi, Mr. Hofstedter," I say, doing my best to hide the polish on my nails.

His eyes flit towards them.

"I love that color," he whispers.

He throws me a good-natured smile before strolling to the front of the class. As he does, he rolls each sleeve of his oxford into matching, elbow-length cuffs.

"I think that's everyone," he says, surveying the room. He ticks off a few names on his clipboard and slips the pen into a blush pink pocket. "Welcome to English."

"Gaaaaaayyyyy," the foghorned insult flies.

A husky chuckle erupts from the front of the class, where Beef Boy slumps in his desk like a giant in a Prius. I don't know if he is talking about me or about Mr. Hofstedter, or both. A sly look back at me makes me think the former.

"*Are you*, Mr. Ainsley?" Mr. Hofstedter retorts. "I'll be honest, I had my suspicions."

Beef Boy snorts a *no* before sinking into his desk silently.

The teacher smirks and winks at me before brushing past the insult like an obnoxious bystander.

"Alright," he says. "Did everyone remember their copy of *Hamlet*?"

"Mr. Weber, do you mind staying back a moment?"

I stop halfway out the door, halting mid-escape. I turn around and walk toward the teacher without a word.

Mr. Hofstedter treads to the door and nudges it nearly

closed before gesturing to the front row.

"Have a seat," he says, chewing on a nail.

I comply, dropping my bag on the floor.

"How are your liking Maple Middle so far?" he asks innocuously.

I shrug.

"It's school," I tell him.

He nods like he hears, but his lack of response makes it clear that was not the question he kept me to ask.

"Good, good," he says. He stumble into the next sentence. "You know, I've noticed you're not like the boys around here."

A knife to the gut. *Is he just going to make fun of me, now, too?* I take a deep breath and ready my defense, a story I kept sharp about how my nonexistent sister had convinced me to let her paint my nails the night before and I had forgotten to remove it before school.

"I—"

Mr. Hofstedter waves a gentle hand to stop me. He stops chewing his nail and leans back on the edge of his desk, arms crossed.

"You know, I understand," he says, all fatherly. "I didn't say that as a reprimand."

I don't know what to say, so I don't. The lanky teacher takes that as an invitation to continue.

"When I was your age," he says, "I was a lot like you. While all the other boys gruffed up and joined the football team, I stayed soft and read my books, drew my drawings. I got made fun of for it, too. Back then, the word was *fudge packer.*"

He says it quietly, almost with reverence. My heart stutters. I think I know where this is going, and I want to stop it as soon as I can.

"I'm not gay," I tell him.

He uncrosses his arms and waves both hands at me.

"No no no no," he says, "of course not. And neither am I."

I can't tell if it's my imagination or not, but I think I see Mr. Hofstedter wink as punctuation to the phrase. He thinks we share a secret.

"I'm really not," I say.

"Exactly," he says, "you're just a little more in touch with your feminine side. I understand completely."

I sigh, nearly certain that Mr. Hofstedter doesn't understand at all.

"I'm just trying to help," he continues.

I let him mutter on, his conversation a stone rolling down a self-built hill.

"Around here, people aren't as open-minded as they are where you're from. I know, I used to live there, too. But here, folks are a little behind the times. They like to think there's a way every man should be and a way every woman should be." He takes my silence as curiosity and continues. "Now, we both know that's not the case, but it's a lot better for everybody if people like you and me play ball with their little fantasy. Is it okay for boys to wear nail polish? Ab-so-*lute*-ly. Is it the best idea to do so in public? Maybe not at Maple Middle."

He steeples his fingers and looks at me through them before sighing, perhaps unable to read the blankness on my face.

"Do you understand what I'm saying?"

After a moment, I slowly nod, more in disbelief that this is happening than from any enlightenment he provides. Mr. Hofstedter springs onto his loafers and gives my shoulder a consolatory squeeze.

"Good."

I stare at the drawing etched in the desktop. It depicts a large, round stick figure fucking a skinny one doggy-style. The skinny figure wears glasses not unlike Mr. Hofstedter's.

"Hey, hey, hey," the teacher says. His voice gets quiet, gets gentler. "It's *okay* to be different. I'm different, too. Just, you know, keep it to yourself, and we'll all get along."

I look into the English teacher's oversized lenses, tempted to tell him just where he can keep it. Behind the glasses, his brown eyes are blurred, as if he is recounting all the times he has had to just keep it to himself, as if he is trying to hide the pain of hiding. How many men had he loved and lost? How hard must it be to keep yourself a secret for so many years? What kept him here, both Maple Middle, and the world at large? But I close my mouth and nod.

"Thank you," I say.

Then, I pick up my backpack and leave.

When I reach the door to my second period history class, I keep going. I'm in such a rush to get anywhere else that my backpack bounces against my spine so hard I'm sure it'll bruise. But the unimportant pain of it does nothing to ease the skullfull of steam brewing in my brain. Mr. Hofstedter's attempt at advice was a burner set to boil, and it succeeded. I don't doubt that he was trying to be helpful, and it's not for me to judge his decision to hide his homosexuality under lock and key. After all, coming out back then had to be even harder than it is now. What makes me mad, though is the assertion that I was *just like him*, doomed to either live the lonely life as a spinster queen or be shunned.

I'm not sure what I am, but I know it's not that.

It was always made clear that I was not one of the boys. I'd long since gotten used to being picked last, to waiting to use the bathroom until it was empty lest I become jockfodder. Even so, all the times I had been called gay, the word had never stuck. My crushes have come in all shades, all shapes, and *gay* is too concrete a thing for that. It doesn't explain the polish, the priss with which I walk. To me, these aren't things that show you who I want to go to bed with, they show you who I want to go to bed as.

I picture Mr. Hofstedter unlocking the door to his one-bedroom apartment every night, shutting the door behind him and breathing freely for the first time that day. I don't want to be like that, a parrot dressed up as a goose, and the teacher's implication that I had to be set me off.

3

———

I steam through the two blue doors at full speed. A teacher calls after me, but I ignore him and jet down the sidewalk.

It takes a few blocks of fastwalking to burn off the bile. I stop to see where I am, realizing I had no idea of a destination. I'd steered hard left out of Maple Middle and was now pointed towards the town's center. Instinct tells me my house is on the other side of it, and I pull out my phone to check the route on my map. Luckily, I'm right. The walk home will take about thirty minutes, meaning I should get back before anyone else. Mom runs errands in the morning, and she isn't usually back till early afternoon. Long enough in any case for me to build an alibi.

I follow the sidewalk into the cluster of buildings masquerading as downtown. Back in the day, it would've been everything you need. Post office, groceries, a bar. Outside the latter, an old man glares over his unfiltered cigarette as I pass. His cheeks are blushed with daydrunk, and he mumbles something incoherent but venomous. I ignore the man and avert my gaze to the sign above him that glows dull yellow in the early autumn gray. *Tootsie's,* it tells me, *A place for one, a place for all.* I'm too far from drinking age to consider walking in, but I don't have difficulty imagining the stares I'd collect from the Coors crowd. Place for all, my ass. Place for the small town conservative, more like.

Further down, the community center stands stoically empty, waiting for kids to get out of school and come to their extracurricular events. Large green letters spell out *Evergreen Community Center*, with a copse of realistic trees replacing the *t* in *Community*. An older woman sits at the bus stop in front. Her small eyes deflate as they falter on me, the squeak of my shoe alerting her to my presence. I know that look too well. It's the one that asks what the world's come to, the one that believes people like me will destroy everything our forefathers built.

I cast my gaze to the ground and push towards home. It's always been like this. Something in how I look makes me the scapegoat for society's sins. Whether I've wanted to or not, I embody everything my elders despise. I don't even need to say a word, just show my face. The face that's not cornfed enough, the hands that are too slight, the hips that wiggle when I walk, the hair that falls longer than a boy's should. These things condemn me to a life outside the lines before I can even open my mouth.

What am I that is so wrong?

My legs tremble tiredly as I walk up to the front door of my house, digging the spare key from under the mat to let myself in. It's silent inside, and darker than outdoors despite the season. I breath in the still air and sigh. It smells safe. No matter where I've been in life, I've always felt better when I'm surrounded by walls. It keeps the bad out. Though it also keeps the bad in, I suppose.

I think of what Mr. Hofstedter said. I don't want to end up like him, hidden away in the midst of middle age. But, spent as

I am of the world at large, I decide maybe hiding another day won't hurt.

I replace the key and lock the door behind me, making my way slowly up the stairs and into my room. I close my eyes and shut the door behind me, doing my best to shudder off the sad.

It doesn't work.

Without fighting it, I fall to the floor and slide out my secret shoebox. I find the bottle of my favorite shade and throw it. The smashing sound it makes lightens my sadness, but the ache in my chest still throbs with every heartbeat. Maybe I imagine it, but the wallpaper around me seems to pulse with it. I listen to the river-rush of blood through my veins, then look at the bits of shattered glass glinting beside me.

It's too much temptation.

I stroke the skin of my cutting arm hungrily, tracing the tracks left from yesterday's damage. The reminder of pain inflames me, and I reach for the shards on the floor. I pick up the biggest and brightest gem, holding it like a slasher's knife, a sharp edge that promises blood to come.

Do you understand what I'm saying? By which he meant, *hide yourself if you seek safety.*

The conversation with Mr. Hofstedter makes my skeleton wants to shed its skin. There is something inside that needs to come out, but what will happen if I let it?

I sit down on the edge of my mattress, racking my brain for the unfindable answer. In frustration, I squeeze my fingers into fists. The hand that holds the shard burns as the broken glass cuts into my palm. The pain sears my synapses, sealing in the sorrow and replacing it with instinct. Now, I am only an animal, and animals don't answer questions. They're just things that bleed. Wetness warms my cheeks. I grip the glass tighter and let it all out before tracing one of the red marks on my forearm. One stroke to strip the scab, one to reopen the wound, and my veins cry red.

A tearing sound tells me that the wall mirrors my masochism. Again, a gash has opened in the dingy floral print. I try to push it from my mind, whatever this illusion is.

Two more cuts to make it bleed, then two more.

My forearm pours, and I feel dizzy but whole. All memory of the conversation with Mr. Hofstedter melts away, leaving only the dull burn of the cuts.

"Hello?"

I hear a voice like butterscotch, sweet and warm with a bite.

Who?

My mind flicks back to the pale eyes I had seen in the wall last night.

That wasn't real, was it?

"Is anyone there?"

I ignore the question, dragging the shard across my arm four more times. Yesterday's wounds open and pour. Wallpaper falls like leaves and I see a glimpse of something like skin.

Okay, what if this is real?

I picture the possibility that she is stuck somehow. Maybe her question is a cry for help, and her only hope is ignoring the sound of her own voice.

"Hello?" she repeats. "I can see you!"

I look up, glimpsing the same pale eyes I saw the night before.

The night before, when I had also cut myself, and this had also happened.

Is me cutting myself opening some sort of portal in the wall? Is this some strange ghost story?

Whatever it is, there is a girl stuck in my wall, and what would it say of me if I didn't let her out? These acts of self-harm are gregarious, necessary for this girl to get out.

I cut myself faster and harder, and the wallpaper tears away in bigger and bigger swathes. The skin of my forearm reminds me of a map of the rivers of Washington, and I trace each tributary from memory. The tear in the wall opens wider and wider, revealing a face, and then a torso, and then a pair of spindly legs growing out of a skirt.

I frame my cuts with the Columbia, a large and deep river that borders the map. The opening crumbles open, and the girl clomps out of the wallspace in a pair of chunky, black combat boots. I fall back on my bed, dizzy from the loss and satisfied that I had done my good deed for the day.

"Hi!" the girl says, as if someone emerging from your wall were an everyday occurrence.

I sit up, almost angry at her nonchalance.

"Where the fuck did you come from?"

The girl giggles as if the question is absurd. A bit taller and older than me, she's dressed like she's headed to a house show. She wears a black dress that could be easily mistaken for an oversized T-shirt, its skirt splattered with rips and holes. Thrown over her shoulders is a large flannel shirt, something from a thrift store, patterned with oil stains I imagine aren't hers. Pale legs sprout from her dress haphazardly, and the boots she wears are creased and worn. I recognize some of her features. She almost looks like a cousin of mine, but I don't know any of my cousins well enough to pinpoint who. Her hair grows over her shoulders like willow leaves, it's hue blandly brown, and her dark brown eyes are flecked with tones of green.

She's attractive, I realize, and I feel myself flush.

"Inside the wall," she tells me in a *duh* sort of way. "Are you okay?"

I respond with a confused look, which she counters with a nod at my arm.

"Oh," I say, my dizziness rekindled at the sight of my own blood. "Yeah, I think so."

The girl walks over to me and crouches to examine my wounds.

"Can I?" she asks.

I nod.

Her hands are cool and damp. I wonder if this is a side effect of residing inside wallspaces or if she just runs cold. When she stands up, she sloughs off her flannel, releasing a heady perfume like flowers kissed with clove. I inhale, and the smell makes me feel slightly better. The girl wraps my bleeding arm in her flannel, ties the sleeves to keep the pressure.

"I would leave that on for a bit," she tells me. "Those cuts are pretty bad."

I nod.

"I was worried you were stuck somehow," I try to explain, "When I saw that my cuts opened the wall, I had to try and get you out."

She smirks at my weak attempt at chivalry, seeing it for the ill-fitting suit it is. Then she extends her hand, purple-painted nails sparkling in the sunlight.

"I'm Violet," she tells me. "What's your name?"

"Oh," I shrug, "I don't know."

"You don't know?" Violet laughs like lavender. "Is that why I hear you crying every night?"

Maybe it was a joke, but the bluntness shocks me silent. After a moment, I shake my head.

"Then what should I call you?"

I scroll through my brain for an answer, my finger landing

on a nickname my mother had given me as a child. She had started by calling me her little VW, my initials, then it evolved.

"Bug, I guess."

"Okay. Bug, then," Violet smiles. "Why have you been crying every night?"

If I hadn't lost so much blood, I imagine I'd be blushing.

"You can hear that?"

"I can hear everything," she says, pointing back at the wall. "I live very close."

There are too many questions to even begin asking.

"Well?"

I push the air from my lungs, and try to blink it all away. It doesn't work. I am still here, and so is Violet. Whatever is going on won't just vanish, whether I want it to or not.

I'd never made a habit of talking about my feelings, as any attempt to would end up with me sputtering or screaming about something that seemed trivial or embarrassing once it was out. But something about Violet draws me in, much like these walls, and makes me want to share everything with her.

"It's just this place," I tell her.

"This place? Like this house?"

I had expected Violet to nod along at my narrative without really engaging. I had always been good at inference, the things I say vague enough that most folks fill in the blanks with whatever they want to hear. *I'm in a bad place* is much easier to hear than *I have feelings inside that I don't understand, and I know they're important, and I really want to get to the bottom of them so I can get on with living in whatever way I choose.* In my experience, nobody cares to listen to an honest answer, so I rarely bother with one. But this girl wants specifics. She wants the facts, if her genuine concern is any indication. I decide to stumble further through my thoughts.

"I mean, this place, this town," I say, "it all feels wrong."

"Wrong how?"

"Wrong, like I don't belong here. Like I'm in the wrong place."

"You don't like it here?" Violet asks.

"It's not that I don't like it," I tell her. "It's just that."

I stop. *Do I even know what it is?*

"Just that what?"

Violet pokes me in the side, and I squirm. I'm not used to familiarity this fast.

"I don't know," I say. "In the city, I felt like I could be myself, and no one really cared who or what I was. Everyone was too caught up in their own shit to notice me. That was nice, in a lonely kinda way."

"But not here?" Violet asks.

"I don't know," I sigh.

We sit silent for a moment, then I continue.

"It's like this place is a blue button-up shirt," I tell her. "There's nothing wrong with a blue button-up shirt, but that doesn't mean it's what I want to wear."

Violet smirks at my analogy, chuckling as she speaks.

"What do you want to wear?"

I flop back on my mattress and scoff. I stare at the ceiling, tracing the terrain of the stucco with my eyes.

"It was a metaphor," I snap.

I feel the mattress sink as Violet sits down beside me.

"You know," she says. "If you're sick of this place, you can always come visit me."

I chuckle.

"You mean in the walls?"

I say it like a joke, still unsure where this girl fits into my reality. But she nods seriously.

This is getting crazy, and my brain feels like it's starting to fry. I clamp my eyelids shut, trying to cool it down.

"Yeah," Violet says. I feel her weight lift from the mattress. "It's not much, but I think you might like it. It's a change, in any case."

"Okay," I say, in the *okay, whatever* way you do when someone sounds crazy. "Maybe some time."

Outside, I hear the crunch of tires on our gravel driveway. A door slams, then a series of smaller crunches as my mother makes her way to the door. The keys click against the nob, and I hear her walk inside.

"Looks like Mom's here," Violet says.

"Mom?" I ask.

"You know, like your female parent," Violet laughs.

Without warning, my bedroom door whooshes open. My mom stands in the open doorway, grocery bags still in hand. She looks around like she's lost. I freeze, afraid that she is going to ask me who this strange girl in my room is.

"Why are you home already?" Mom's eyes narrow. "And who are you talking to?"

I look to Violet for an answer, but I am alone in the room. Before I can speak, my mom gasps and the grocery bags fall to the floor with a metal-on-glass crash. Her eyes flit from the broken bottle on the ground to my bleeding forearm to the glass shard in my hand. In the whirl of it all, I had nearly forgotten about my wounds.

"What *happened*?" Mom hisses.

She says it in a way that tells me she doesn't want a response, let alone the truth. Then she rushes into the room and yanks me off my bed by my bleeding arm. The firmness of her movement knocks Violet's flannel off of my arm. I reach for the fabric like it's a life raft, but it slips past my fingers.

"Come *here*."

With no other option, I follow her to the bathroom as listlessly as a tin can tied to a bicycle.

4

—————

"What *happened*?" my mom echoes, while I ask myself the same thing.

It's obvious Mom didn't see Violet, or she would have surely commented on the strange older girl in my bedroom.

Did I even see Violet?

The certainty I had discovered only minutes ago dispels, and met with empiric fact, I have to wonder if I saw anything at all. I mean, if anyone told me that a random girl emerged from their bedroom wall, I know what I'd think. I can't help but picture myself locked in a room and secured to a bed while a parade of practitioners evaluate my existence.

Maybe there's something wrong with me.

My mom squeaks on the bathtub tap and turns it to luke-warm. With all the care of construction worker, she grabs my bloody arm and runs it under the splatter. The old-pipe rushing sounds like the ocean, and for a moment I'm calmed by the simplicity of the sound. I finally fling out a fumbled response to my mom's question.

"I was painting my nails, and I dropped the bottle," I tell her.

It's enough of a confession to lend it some spine, while still letting me hold my cards close. I can't tell her about Violet, not until I know what's really going on. I'd heard what happens to kids whose parents send them to get psychiatric help. The parents' word is always law. Kids can never plead their case.

"The cuts?" she asks expectantly.

"I tripped when I was cleaning it up."

A moment of silence as Mom calculates the validity of this explanation. After a minute, the sharp edges of her expression melt away. For now, she's accepted my story. Or at least she thinks it's simpler to stomach than the truth.

She washes the cuts on my arm with careful pats from a palmed bar of soap. Once she is satisfied with her work, she turns off the tap and dries my arm with a hand towel before pulling open a drawer and raking through it.

"Sit down," she tells me.

I lower myself onto the toilet cover, wincing as the air cools my raw slices. Mom finds the bandages she was looking for and kneels in front of me, motioning for my arm. I give her what she wants. She peels the backing off a bandage and carefully places it over the first cut.

"School's not out for hours."

Not a question, but it might as well be.

"Oh, uh," I stumble, "there was a gas leak in the school, and they had to evacuate us for the day."

I don't know much about gas leaks, other than the fact that those two words are always spoken with fear and reverence. I mentally cross my fingers, hoping that my second story of the hour will stick. My mom's crinkled brow tries to fill in a few holes, but whether or not she can, she moves onto the next question.

"How's school going?" she asks me.

I shrug, pulling hard at the arm she's captured. I wish Violet was here. I would tell her everything.

"Everybody just seems to ignore me, which is fine as far as I'm concerned."

"So you walked home?"

"Yeah," I tell her. "I used Maps. It didn't take too long."

"You should've called me."

"It's fine, Mom, we're not in the city anymore."

"True," she concedes, "but it's a new place, and I don't want you to get lost."

"I'll call next time," I sigh.

My mom peels the backing off a final bandage and covers the last cut. She examines her work before releasing my arm. Then she grabs my hand.

"Vernon?" she asks.

I nod.

"You would tell me if something was wrong, right? If you were cutting yourself for some reason?"

She's letting her cards slip. I make a mental note that I'll have to be more careful.

"I tripped, Mom," I insist.

"I know, but," she says, "if you were doing something like that, you know you can tell me, right? I know kids can be mean."

Her final phrase insinuates a knowledge of me I wasn't sure she possessed. I suppose it's obvious that I'm far from the ideal American boy, but I have to wonder if she has the same suspicions about myself that I do.

"I know," I say. "I really did trip, though. School is fine. Everyone leaves me alone."

The brevity of my clauses shuts her up. She lets go of my hand and sighs, accepting the loss. I don't know if it's the light, but her eyes look waterlogged.

I smile at her to show her that everything really is as fine as I say it is. She smiles back and stands up, walking out of the bathroom.

"Please, don't play with the bandages," she says. "I'll be in the kitchen. Dinner will be in a bit."

The sound of her steps recedes down the stairs.

I walk across the hall into my room. The afternoon light shines through my window, revealing the room's emptiness. The wall from which Violet had emerged is once again whole, though it is plastered with a sickly white paste that clashes with the wallpaper. Were there anyone else here, there's no way they could've fixed it in the five minutes I was gone. I place my palm against the fix, attempting to dispel the mirage, but it's solid. My eyes well. I know I need someone now but going to Mom is not an option. Violet would've helped, I'm sure, but now she's gone again.

My shoes crunch up the broken bits of bottle lying on the floor. Mom was so scattered after seeing my cuts she had forgotten to clean it up. Or maybe she wanted me to, as a sort of punishment for not letting her in on the truth.

As I kneel down to pick up the pieces, my water mixes with the purple polish spill. Something under my bed catches my eye. I reach underneath and pull out the flannel that Violet had wrapped my arm with. The bloodstains are drying and have started to crust. I put the fabric to my face and breath in the perfume. It fills my lungs, and bit by bit, I begin to feel whole again.

5

———

Imagine this is your story, instead of mine.

If you were a kid in ill-fitting skin, wouldn't you, too, try cut out the sad?

If against all expectation, you found a friend, someone who accepted the extraordinary truth of you, wouldn't you tell her everything?

It wouldn't even matter if she was a ghost, a figment, a freak like you.

And when your mother finds you, sobbing into the air with a shard in your hand, would open your wounds to her? Or would you crawl into a crevice like the shameful creature you are, letting your cascading cuts bleed you of your woes?

If by grace you were cleansed of your grief and your sins were bandaged, would it be enough to stop you from looking lustfully at the broken glass on the ground?

Of course, if you were a boy, you'd take as deep a breath as your body allows, and on the exhale, you'd breathe out all memory of ghosts, girls in walls, and well-meaning-but-closeted English teachers.

If you were a boy, you'd squeeze away the tears because

boys don't cry. Nor do they talk to imaginary girls, or paint their nails, or entertain the ramblings of a sad, sequestered queen in the hopes that's there's a hidden hint of truth in what he tells you that maybe, just maybe, will unlock the closet you've been trying to crawl out of.

And if you were a boy, with your feelings fully repressed, you'd (carefully, now) pick up the pieces of glass on the floor, appreciating silently the metaphor of what you are doing.

You'd home these broken pieces in a plastic bag, tie it closed, and take it outside to where the garbage barrel leans languidly against the curb, putting the whole thing to rest as you close the lid over your shame.

If you were a boy, you'd go back inside, collect a bowl and a towel, and fill the bowl with warm water before taking a knee down like you're getting before god to clean the floorboards of your violet secrets. And with your hard-earned forgiveness, you'd go about the day with all the smile you can savvy, greeting every last god-blessed human, dog, and cat you encounter, as if only hours ago you weren't crying at a ghost, cut of your own hand.

The first night would be the hardest, sure, haunted by the memory of what happened while the sun was up. When the walls start to thump like the beat of your heart, her little fists pounding to get out, you'd plug your earbuds into your phone and turn up your favorite podcast to drown it all out.

Maybe, you would even sleep.

And the next day, when the sun streams in the window to illuminate the glorious nothing-but-a-normal-bedroom, you would smile and sigh and tell yourself that this is the first day of the rest of your normal, normal life.

If this was your story, and if you were a boy, you'd live the rest of your days in relative comfort, knowing normality for the goldmine you'd been gifted.

But it's not your story, it's mine.

And I'm not so sure I'm a boy anymore.

As I cry over the remains of my favorite bottle of *Sally Hansen Insta-Dry* nail polish, the freshly cleaned cuts on my arm begin to burn with that familiar urge. They beg me to open them again, to let it all out. They remind me that, no, I am not normal, and couldn't be if I tried. They remind me of the *faggot* chorus I was serenaded with this morning, of Mr. Hofstedter's condescending attempt at protecting a child from the life of an outsider. They remind me that there's a reason I've chosen to cut myself, as opposed to the thousands of other ways I could lull myself into a blissful state of dissociation. They remind me that with every stroke of glass against skin, I'm excavating, digging past the surface to find the person I know is underneath.

I don't clean up the mess. I don't take it to the trash and sweep it under the rug for the rest of my days. I don't lead a normal, normal life.

As I search for the shard that will be my shovel, my eyes well up with the wish that this story did belong to someone else. I watch myself, powerless to stop as I peel the bandages, so carefully placed moments ago, off my arm. The slices have already begun to scab, but I will not let them heal. I drag the glass across each red line, with the precision and purpose of a surgeon holding a scalpel. One by one, the cuts pour fresh red, drops falling onto the purple stain on the floor. Little by little, the sadness is replaced by pain, and pain I can handle. When I have opened all the cuts, I count them. Thirteen, one for each of my years. Like an eager student, I multiply. I cross each line with another, creating thirteen skinny X's that weep in my stead. My pulse excites as I hear the wallpaper ripping off, scrap by scrap. The plaster crumbling open to reveal all my secrets.

"Bug!"

I hear the footsteps, then feel the slender arms of Violet wrap me round and pull me to my feet. I smell her perfume, like chai brewing in a field of flowers, and I lean into my only hope. She is surprisingly strong, seeming to support me with little effort. She holds me tight, silently, while I cry into her oversized flannel. Her shoulder soaks up my sad, and I mumble apologies that go unacknowledged.

"Do you wanna come with me for a bit?" she says, sounding the way a mother should sound.

I nod.

As I lean against her, she leads me towards the opening in the wall. I let her guide me, my face still buried in her softness. Though my eyes are closed, I feel the air cool as we enter the wallspace. I smell the must, a not-unpleasant, muddy scent. Like the perfume of Earth herself. I feel the light drain around me, replaced by the dusky dim of secret spaces.

I'm shocked to realize that I trust this strange girl, almost implicitly.

As I breathe her in and nuzzle into her clothes, she leads me out of my world and into hers.

6

As we step into the wall, my foot catches an edge, and Violet catches me before I fall.

I drag my eyes from their hiding place in Violet's shoulder so that I'm not completely useless. With a squeeze on my arm, she says *I'm still here if you need me.*

The coolness of the air pricks at my skin, waking me with every step further into the wallspace. Fluffy pink wallguts stain my nostrils with a chemical-sweet scent, while all around me dusty webs drape the studs that support the walls, while their timid tenants eight-eye the newcomer. This is the kind of place skeletons slump in old horror movies, a place where secrets are kept secluded from sight. As Violet leads me further into the dark, I wonder if I should really be here. My head buzzes for me to stop, to turn around and return to my room. Maybe I'm not yet a lost cause. Maybe this can all be forgotten.

For a moment, my steps falter.

Violet senses my hesitation.

"Just a bit farther," she says.

She points down the darkness to where the wall turns a

corner. With a gentle tug, she asks if I want to follow. I let her guide me toward it, leaving behind everything I've been told to be with every foot further. Warm light hints at something better around the bend, and I smell hints of something like cinnamon.

Soon, the source of the light becomes visible. Around the corner, a doorway is filled warm, pinkish light, like the glow of a stained-glass lamp. It spills out of the door, splashing the walls with color. The closer we get to the doorway, the cleaner the walls become. The cobwebs have disappeared, and the puritanical studs that greeted me in the entrance are hidden with floral wallpaper that matches what's in my room. The same purple buds sprout from vines and weave cursive circles across the walls. When I lean in to look, the blooms bless me with the smell of chai. It sends tingles down my spine, and I pause to steep in the feeling.

"Cool, huh?" Violet asks.

She lets go of my arm as she does, leaving me to support my own weight.

"They smell so pretty," I say to her, eyes following the floral trails.

Violet smiles.

"Ready?" she says.

I answer by following her towards the doorway, now ten yards away. The pinkish light emanating from it warms on my face, a feeling like stepping inside after walking miles in the cold. A small mew calls my attention to the floor. The dusty wood I had stood on before is now thick carpet, and the soles of my feet sink into it gratefully. Plush animals and pillows haunt the hallway outside the door like the overflow of a crowded club. Among the plush, a few furry curls lounge languidly. One yawns, showing me friendly fangs. Its green eyes jump out of the orange, blacks and white of its calico as it mews a lazy greeting. Beside me, Violet responds with her own version of its language. Satisfied that I'm alright, the cat lays its chin on its paws and blinks blandly.

"He's Otto," Violet tells me. "Short for Ottoman. Can you guess why?"

Curled up, the cat shows his size. He is larger than most I have seen, and his braided body looks cozy enough to rest your feet on. I giggle.

"I think so," I say. "He's adorable. Can I pet him?"

I'm almost embarrassed by my overeagerness, but the temptation to touch the cuddly cat outshines the bad. My family had never had pets, leaving my creaturely needs sorely malnourished.

Violet nods.

I crouch down and tentatively stretch my hand out towards the snoozing kitty. As I do, the dim light illuminates the cuts I've collected on my forearm. I retract my arm before reaching out the other. Otto acknowledges me by opening his eyes halfway and regarding my hand with disinterest. I pet the fur that sprouts from his spine, and he closes his eyes, making a small motorous noise.

"He's sassy, but he's a sweetheart," Violet says.

"How many cats do you have?" I ask her, glancing around at the two or three others in view. They lounge or lick themselves, keeping close to the walls.

Violet laughs as if I asked something stupid.

"I don't own them," she says. "But there's thirteen of them."

"Thirteen?" I'd never heard of so many cats being in one place. "If they're not yours, who's are they?"

Violet shrugs.

"As far as I know, they don't belong to anyone any more than you or I do," she tells me. "We're all just, I dunno. Here."

She says the word *here* as if it explains everything that's going on, though to me it explains nothing. I open my mouth to ask more, but Violet waves me toward her.

"Come on," she says. "Let's clean up those cuts."

As if she spoke the things into existence, my arm starts to throb.

I watch Violet walk into the room, the dull glow making her a slight, beautiful eclipse. Taking one last breath of the wallflower's scent, I stand up and follow her through the door.

Chatter floats from a small television propped up on a black-painted dresser. The subtle glow of the screen illuminates wallfulls of band posters, hand-drawn epithets, and pictures. The people in the posters are dressed in shades of black, eyes inked thickly to show their sorrow. Rips and tears adorn denim and leather jackets chocked with patches sewn on with floss.

I remember seeing people like this in the city. Gutterpunks and castaway kids wearing their sadness on their sleeves. I'd always felt a connection with them, though I had never found myself a part of their crowd. Maybe I was too timid to introduce myself, or maybe I was too afraid of what the world would think of me to join their ranks. But as my eyes frolic through the images on the wall, I feel a retrospective kinship with these outcasts, as if, all along, I've been one of them in spirit. My skins feels suddenly tight, like a cocoon ready to burst. Something inside me is begging to be released.

Amid the posters are a few framed photos. My eyes are drawn to a small black frame holding a Polaroid of a girl laying languidly on a mess of sheets. She's wearing only a tee, and with one hand she pulls the hem down, secreting away whatever shame lies beneath. The other arm halos her hair-drenched head, a network of thin, white stripes scarring its skin. My blood rushes with wanting, and I wonder who was lucky enough to photograph this softcore soliloquoy.

"Do you like Wobble?" Violet asks me.

When she sees my confused expression, she motions at one of the posters near the photo I was shamefully staring at. It depicts a group of androgynous punks with dyed-pink hair draped in oversize flannels. The name Wobble seems too happy for their stern expressions.

"Uh, I dunno them," I stumble.

I pray she didn't see me slobbering over the half-naked woman on her wall. Something tells me it's a picture of her. I ask the first thing that comes to mind, hoping to move the focus elsewhere.

"What show is this?"

I point at the TV, though the motion is hardly necessary. When I do, my cuts gleam in the glow as if they had just been made.

"Let's get those taken care of," Violet says, grabbing my arm and directing me to sit on the bed. "It's called *Mayberry*. It's kind of a sappy show about a mother and daughter in a small town, but I like watching it. It makes me feel, I dunno, at home kinda."

As she speaks, she rumbles through a couple drawers, finding first a purple plastic package then a roll of gauze.

"I'm not really set up for first aid here," she says, "but I think these face wipes will work wonders on cleaning up those cuts."

She walks over to her bed and plops the items onto the raggled sheets. Adjusting one of her pillows so that it's propped against the wall, she reaches for a blanket draped off the side of the mattress. With a pat on the pillow, she instructs me to lay back. I comply.

"May I?" she asks, holding up the blanket.

I nod, eager for the comfort of coverage.

"Keep your arm out so I can clean it up," she says. She

starts to wipe it clean before asking, "What do you do to be nice to yourself?"

I spend a moment searching for the answer.

"Oh, I don't know," I tell her.

"I think on hard days it's important to do something nice for yourself." She makes eye contact with me. "It seems like maybe you've had one of those."

She gives me space to respond. I almost argue, tell her that I'm just fine, thanks, but then I catalog the day's dreariness.

"It was a pretty shit day," I concede.

Violet nods.

"I thought so," she says. "Well, what helps me on pretty shit days is taking a little time to do something I enjoy, guilt-free. Maybe that means cozying up with your favorite show, or maybe that means pampering yourself in some way. Makeup, nails, a face mask." She pauses, wiping clean a particularly goopy slice. "It doesn't seem like you've been too nice to yourself today."

I bristle before my eyes well up. I brush them dry with my good arm.

"It was a pretty shit day," I repeat.

Violet hums agreement.

"I'm so sorry, Bug," she says somberly. "What if I helped you do something nice for yourself?"

My throat swells closed.

"That would be great," I say.

Violet smiles.

"Well since it's been a shitty day," she says. "What if I pamper you a bit? It looks like these nails could stand a new coat. You can cozy up and watch *Mayberry* while I paint them."

Rarely had I ever taken time to do only things that made me happy. The prospect of it made me uncomfortable, like I was somehow giving into a selfish bent I had been told to ignore. Who was I to deserve this sort of special treatment? I'd only been used to the opposite, to self-punishment, not self-care. I wipe at a tear that slides down my cheek.

"That actually sounds really, really nice," I say.

Violet traces the cleaned-up cuts on my forearm with a perfectly painted nail. My skin tingles as she does.

"Hey, Bug," she says. "You really did a number on yourself this time. Double digits."

Reflexively, I try to pull my arm back, but she grips it firmly and I cannot get away. I flush with a mixture of embarrassment and panic. I've never been keen on showing my scars. They tell a story I keep stashed away, a story in a language of my own making. But by the way Violet scans down the scant lines scoring me, I can tell she knows how to read it.

"I haven't been doing it for long," I lie.

She begins to wrap my arm in gauze.

"It's okay," she tells me. "I don't judge. But I do hope one day you're able to stop."

My head buzzes, overwhelmed by the vulnerability of the moment. Out of habit, I turn my gaze to the screen and focus on the show instead. On it, the main characters eat lunch at the local diner, discussing The New Boy over hamburgers that haven't gone to their hips. I squint at the screen, trying to transport myself to their town by sheer force of will.

"Bug," Violet says firmly. I half-look her way. She sighs before continuing, "All I'm trying to say is that the world is gonna hurt. Especially for people like us. People will leave you empty and bruised, and the only thing you can do about it is hold tight to the hope that the next day holds something worth having."

I wonder if the glow of the screen makes my tears sparkle. Violet wraps my arm in a second layer of gauze.

"Life will hurt enough without you hurting yourself," Violet tells me.

Her voice has lowered a bit, and her unfocused eyes make it hard to tell if she's talking to me or herself. We both watch silently as Violet wraps my arm in a third layer of beige fabric before snipping off the end. I think of how my mother had been doing the same thing an hour earlier, how her hands had felt drastically different.

Violet stands up and re-homes her supplies in their respective drawers. Neither of us comment on the rattling sounds she's making. Finally, I speak.

"I feel like I don't know what it's like not to hurt."

Violet takes a shaky breath before she dives into another drawer. I hear the familiar clinking of glass on glass. It's the same sound I hear when I'm pawing through my secret shoe-box. Violet turns around with a bottle in hand. The light from the TV makes the glass curves glitter.

"I'm thinking purple for your nails," she says. "That's your favorite color, right?"

"Yeah," I say. "How did you know?"

Violet shrugs and sits back on the bed with her lap facing me. She motions for me to put my hands in it so she can paint them.

As I do, I say, "I've never had my nails painted by someone else before."

"Ooh, girl," Violet replies. "It's the best. Just sit back, get cozy, and watch TV. I'll take care of the rest."

I smile and lean back into the pillow she had propped up for me. Violet takes my hand in hers and begins to paint my nails with slim strokes. Beneath the blanket, my body feels baked, and my muscles turn to hot butter. I startle slightly as one of the cats hops onto the bed and curls up next to me. I hadn't seen this cat before, but I inherently know it's a she. The cozy kitty purrs and wraps her tail around her body.

In that moment, something clicks in my head. The gears that had been off for years fall into place. Violet called me *girl,* without me asking her to. I'd only ever been called boyish things, names like *buddy* and *big guy.* Names that sound condescending by almost anyone that uses them. I knew I was considered a *beta male,* the soft sort that doesn't fit into the ball-tossing crowd. But what I've never understood is why I was considered a male at all, if the shoe so clearly didn't fit. But how do you tell someone, anyone, to stop calling you the name you've been given?

Somehow Violet just knows. She understands that I'm not what I've been told I am. She has felt the weight of being born into a life you didn't ask for.

It feels good being called *girl.* It feels right.

Lounging on Violet's purple bed, watching *Mayberry* while she paints my nails, I feel at home for the first time.

I feel myself.

I feel like a girl.

7

Violet puts the last stroke of purple on my pinky, then blows it dry.

She looks up and smiles.

"Feel better?"

I breathe in and out like the tideflow.

"Yeah," I sigh.

"If you really wanna be pampered, we could do a full makeover."

I hesitate.

"It's something I love doing," she says.

I laugh with a sound like the breeze, the idea of a makeover causing equal parts excitement and nerve.

"Okay," I say. "Yeah, let's do it."

Violet leads me to a small stool in front of her vanity and sits me down.

Even though I had painted my nails for years, I had never forayed into the multifaceted world of makeup. To me, the collection of bottles, brushes, and palettes she flourishes a hand over have all the strangeness of alchemical elements kept by a medieval magician. They feel magical, as if they are charged with the power to save me from a life I wish not to live. One by one, Violet opens the bottles and sprays, spreads and brushes their contents onto my face. My skin feels chilly but fresh like dew, like this is a new morning for me.

With a final spritz, Violet stands back and examines her work.

"Lovely," she says.

I turn to look in the mirror, but she stops me.

"First clothes," she implores. "You gotta see the whole look together."

Violet leads me into a dark closet in the corner of the room. She fumbles through the shadows a second before clicking on a light in the middle of the ceiling. The shaky bulb illuminates a trove of clothes fit for any teen goth queen. The many shades of black fabric make me fly with crow's wings. Before me, a collection of oversized flannels and tees frame a decorum of dress in shades of black, gray, purple, and green. Stacks of sweaters sit softly on the shelf above the rack, and the floor features an assortment of boots and sneakers marred by the occasional pair of heels.

"It's incredible," I tell her.

Clothes had always been a necessary evil for me, tasteless things chosen from the wrong side of the aisle. Often, I'd wandered into the women's section while shopping for school clothes, only to be instantly ushered out. I once felt the softness of a pink sweater for a second before my mom's claws found me.

But before me, Violet's closet contains every article I've ever wanted to wear. Each piece of fabric looks like it was made for my body. I flick through the dresses, tracing necklines and testing pockets, then I run my hand across the soft sheets of flannel hanging beside. I bend over to examine a pair of platform heels decorated with tiny spikes.

"Let's start with something a little easier," Violet says. "Can I pick something for you?"

I nod, and she skreeks through the hangers expertly. In moments, she's ensembled an outfit for me to try. She hands me the small pile and walks out of the closet.

"I won't look," she says behind me.

It's merciful, leaving me the only witness to my body. She must understand how it feels to look at yourself with loathing.

I undress and slip into the purple cotton dress she selected. It feels foreign at first, an unexpected sense of freedom as the skirt whirls around me. I twist a bit, getting used to the sensation. Then I slip into the leggings, sweater, and boots she left me. I take a deep breath, preparing myself for the deep end.

"Okay," I tell Violet.

She turns around to look at me.

"You look adorable!" she squeals. "Come here!"

I let her usher me out of the closet.

Violet spins me around in front of the mirror, and I meet myself for the first time. My immediate reaction is to look at everything but my reflection. A habit I'd formed years ago. I examine the backwards image of Violet's room behind me, the snorgling cat on her bed, the flickering glow of the television. I hadn't noticed until I was in front of it, but the mirror is illuminated by a circle of light with no definite source. The border of the mirrorglass glows as if inhabited by fairies.

Violet notices my wandering eyes.

"No," she says, grabbing my shoulders and pointing me at my reflection. "Look at *you!*"

I drag my gaze onto my face, and the floor falls out underneath me. With my slight build and dusty prickle of hair, I look like I could be Violet's younger sister. Still stuck in the awkwardness of pubescence, but a sister, nonetheless. My heart thuds in my ears as I take in my reflection and pick apart the pieces. I had never seen a girl in the mirror, not when I'd looked at myself, but now I know I won't see anything but. I realize that I've spent my life as a puzzle missing pieces. Only now do I see the full picture of me.

"Who is that?" I ask.

It comes across as wit, but the question is genuine. The face in front of me is new, yet altogether familiar. Like a recently remodeled bedroom. Even if it's everything you want, the shock of seeing it is searing. I watch as a tear spills out of the reflection's eye, tracing a vein of mascara down one cheek. Without a word, Violet wipes it away.

"You're so pretty!" she says.

Pretty. The phrase is alien, yet, in this moment, so fitting. I erupt into a fury of giggles that I can't suppress. As someone who rarely even speaks, I can't remember the last time I had gorged on laughter. My body feels made of bubbles, effervescence catching like fire as Violet begins to chuckle behind me. She gives me a hug, cementing our sisterhood. I squeeze her arm affectionately.

"I am kind of pretty," I say.

"Kind of?" Violet retorts. "Girl, you're gorge!"

Connecting the face in the mirror to my own neck takes practice, but as I look in the mirror I see that those are my slight features, my oval jawline. My brows, bold and close to the eye. Violet's work had brought out the best without hiding the truth of who I am. A hazy line over my lids makes my irises ten feet deep. The mascara licking my lashes turns laughable naivete into lovable innocence. The kiss of blush, the pale pink lipstick bring life to dead expression. I shudder as I take it all in. As new as this image is, I've never felt more myself. I start to cry as I realize what that means.

Violet squeezes me harder.

"Do you not like it?" she says, concern prominent in her tone.

"No no no," I tell her. "I love it."

I breathe in flowers and spice, the scent that I now know is the smell of home.

"Thank you," I say.

"No problem, Bug," Violet says.

I pause for a moment. The nickname seems unfit for this new version of me, but since I don't know what to call it, I stay quiet.

"Did you hear that?" Violet asks.

I shake my head as she walks over to the television and clicks it off. Without the mumble of *Mayberry*, I hear what she is referring to.

"Vernon!" my mother says, muted by the layers of plaster between us.

Her voice poisons the peace I am only just discovering. The beautiful face Violet gave me suddenly seems shameful, the few glances I can give it show a young boy painted up like a clown. Instead of comfortable, the dress I am wearing becomes exposing, loose rags on a sick child. I draw my knees up to hold them, relaxing an inch when they block the mirror from my view.

I know Violet is watching. My insecure nature tells me she is angry, disappointed at the thing on her stool that couldn't hold its own weight, a tree broken by snow. But when she strokes my shoulders, I realize she shares my fear. With the compassion of a person witnessing the unjustly jailed, she reaches through my bars and pries my clenched hands out of tense flesh.

"It's okay," she tells me.

I'm not sure I agree, but I appreciate the sentiment, nonetheless.

"Maybe I can stay here," a croaked question cloaked as a statement.

Violet looks uneasy.

"I don't think that's such a good idea," she says, her eyes tracing the bounds of her room.

She seems to want to say more but doesn't. The tendrils choking at me dig themselves into the floor. I don't want to leave here, not yet. I had only just begun to draw an honest picture of myself, just started imagining the places I could go. My mother's calling cuts the warmth of Violet's room with the cold reality of the world outside. It hurts more than any edge I've drug across my skin. I curl further into myself, all of my muscles solidifying into statue. They tremble with the exertion of holding off the darkness creeping around me. My lungs begin to burn, and I realize I have not taken a breath in nearly a minute. I gasp for it, my mouth filling with the sweet hint of flowers and spice. Eyes tight, I dive into the darkness of dissociation, clawing at the cord that tethers me to my body in hopes of cutting it. I float for a moment in nothing, before a pale arm reaches into the black.

"Bug! Hey, Bug!" Violet yells into my ear.

She shakes my shoulders a bit, as if she is rousing me from sleep. I surface from the sea of black gulping at the air like it's a drug. I open my eyes and realize that they are filled with hot water that drip-drops down my face and onto the floor.

"Bug," Violet implores. "It's okay! It's gonna be okay. I'll still be here when you come back."

When you come back.

She says it with a certainty that soothes me a bit. I inhale shakily, a sound like the rattle of old ducts, and breathe out as much of the bad as I can. I know it's still inside, but the breath makes it that much bearable.

"I can come back?" I ask Violet.

"Of course you can! I'm sure I'll see you again. We can watch TV and do whatever you want to do. We'll have a good time."

I nod slowly, not sure if I believe it yet.

"Vernon! Where are you?! If you don't come out here right now, you're in big trouble mister!"

Every word my mother yells hits me like a punch. Defeated for now, I pull away from Violet's embrace. She smiles, though her eyes are shaded with sadness.

"Hey, Bug," she says, following me to the door. "I'll see you soon."

She gives me a tiny push out the door and one last smile. I follow her hint and step into the space between our worlds. I hear a click as she closes the door behind me.

I take a few tentative steps into the dark corridor. There is only one way to go, but I still feel lost as I try to remember when Violet led me down this way earlier. It had to have been, what, only hours ago? But it feels an eternity away. I feel like I've changed more in the past few hours than I have in all of my life combined. Or, maybe not changed, but evolved. Maybe this is growing up, maturing into the person you were always meant to be.

The cold air of the space inside the walls chills me. My legs shiver, and the dress I am still wearing clings to my shuddering hips.

Fuck.

I can't go out there like this. My mom will freak, and almost certainly tell my dad. My parents aren't the kind to hurt me, but they would never look at me the same again. They wouldn't mention it either, but only once they made it damn clear that it will never happen again. In their eyes, I couldn't be a girl, that's not how the world works.

I spin around quickly and hammer on Violet's door.

"Violet! I need my clothes!"

No response.

I knock again, but by the third volley of knocks I know she won't answer. There is no sound coming from the other side of the door, and the space below it is as dark as a closed storefront. The wood of it even feels cold, like it hasn't been touched in forever.

"Vernon!" my mother calls behind me.

I have no choice but to forge ahead. I do my best to push the fear from my mind as I run my hand along the wall, stepping one foot in front of the other as the floral wallpaper turns back to woodslat and plaster. My hand demolishes a spiderweb and I shriek instinctively.

"Vernon, is that you?"

I run the rest of the way to the wall that borders my bedroom. My throat chokes as I realize that the opening has healed over, likely when Violet bandaged my cuts. I feel stupid for not expecting this, stupid for not tying myself down in her room and refusing to leave.

"Vernon, where are you?"

My mom's voice is closer now. I can hear her on the other side of the plaster. She must be in my room.

Taking a deep breath, I brace my forearms over my head and run straight at the sound. Even though my eyes are clenched, I can see the light as I crash through the wall into my bedroom.

I hear a bang like bone on wood.

"Ow! Vernon?"

I open my eyes to see my mother on all fours by the space

under my bed, rubbing her skull. As she blinks away the pain, she sees me. I brace for impact.

"Vernon, where the hell have you been?"

She stands up and crosses her arms.

"Why are you shaking?" she asks. "You're all dusty!"

I wait for the shock of my appearance to abate and for the scary questions to start. *Vernon, why are you wearing a dress? Vernon, is that lipstick? You're a boy, Vernon. Boys don't do this. You're gonna pay for that hole in the plaster!*

My mother says nothing, instead crossing her arms tighter as she waits for my response to her only spoken question.

What?

I look down. The dress I had borrowed from Violet had been replaced with the tee and jeans I was wearing before. I run fingers over my lips and verify that, yes, the lipstick is gone, too. I spin around to see the damage I had done to get back into my room, but there is no sign of my dramatic entrance. The wall is just as solid as the day it was built.

How could that have happened? I know I just broke through. I felt it.

Just to be certain, I feel my hair. Bits of plaster fall from it, and I sense the tangle of cobwebs stuck to it.

"*Well?*" my mom says. "Were you outside?"

I nod, stunned by the shock of everything that had just occurred.

"You're supposed to tell me when you go, Vernon. And don't get your clothes all dirty. It means more work for me."

I stare for a moment.

"I'm sorry," I say.

"Dinner's ready. I'll give you five minutes to clean up and get downstairs. You've made us wait too long. The food'll be cold if it's not already."

All I do is nod.

My mother shakes her head in frustration before uncrossing her arms and walking out of the room.

I begin to shirk my old clothes, my bad clothes, the clothes I don't want. I miss the cling of Violet's dress. Sighing sharply, I collect the pieces of myself and make them as presentable as possible.

8

When I settle into the open seat at the table, my father is already eating. He slops up the pasta with a fork and a spoon, the corners of his mouth carnivore red from the marinara. He looks up when my chair squeaks, though only to shoot me a look of disdain for making him wait for his meal.

"Spaghetti's cold," he says through a half-full mouth.

Even though my mom closes her eyes, I can see them roll. She folds a napkin over her lap and begins to spin the noodles around her fork.

"Did you have fun outside?" she asks before slipping the forkful of food into her mouth, chewing chastely as if she were being watched by the world.

For a moment, I flounder for what she means before remembering my earlier excuse.

"Cold for September," my dad says.

My mom doesn't acknowledge him.

"Oh," I say. "Yeah, I guess."

"Didn't you get cold?" my dad asks.

"Have you made any friends at school?" my mom plows

through. "You said everyone ignores you, but I have a hard time believing that in a town this small."

"Um, there's a teacher who's kinda nice." I remember my conversation with Mr. Hofstedter. The anger I had since turned to pity. "He means well, anyway. Everyone says he's gay."

My heart stops as I mumble the last sentence. I wasn't trying to, but by even uttering that word, I was toeing risky territory. I could use it as a segue, could tell my parents how I've been feeling, the questions I've had. That would be the healthy thing to do, right? The honest thing. I mean, they're my parents, they'd still love me, no matter what. At least they're supposed to.

"Gay," my dad scoffs like it's a punchline. He snorts so hard I expect spaghetti to slink out his nose.

"Don't be a child, Peter," my mom says. She turns to me, "Vernon, I'm sure he's not actually gay. Kids say all sorts of mean things."

Oh, I know, trust me.

"Mean? Is it so bad to be gay?"

The question speaks itself. Never one to rock the boat, I fear that even such a tame jab at my parent's addiction to the norm could be seen as a provocation.

My dad makes a face like his spaghetti has turned to worms, though he continues to shovel it into his gob despite. My mom just looks down and carefully collects more noodles on her fork.

"School called," she tells me. "About your absence."

She is silent a moment, seemingly expecting a response. I give her nothing.

"There was no gas leak."

Fuck.

I guess I should be thankful such a shit story kept for that long, but I'm so nervous I put down my fork, unused.

"You lied to me," my mom says. "You skipped all your classes after first period."

My dad's utensils shush for a moment before continuing their cacophony.

You lied to me, my head says in the voice of my mother. *You're a faggot. A little homo ladyboy. Mr. Hofstedter told me all about it. No wonder you two get along. Couple of queers, quite the pair.*

I pick up my fork to silence myself with spaghetti, but my appetite dies alongside the boldness I felt moments ago.

"I didn't feel good."

My mom sees through the lie, she has to. I can hear the gears in her brain clicking as they count the inconsistencies I've been throwing her like a shitty accountant. She takes a bite of pasta, a possible sign, I hope, she can't quite solve the sum. She swallows before speaking.

"You can tell me if something's wrong, Vernon."

My heckles go up.

I really can't.

"I know," I say, with more force than I feel. "My stomach is gross. I'm gonna go to my room."

Without waiting for permission, I stand up and walk away, leaving my chair carelessly untucked. As I take the steps up, I hear my dad cough into his plate, silverware clinking chaotically.

My mom sighs, a deep and long sound that reminds me of a cold winter wind rushing through the forest outside.

❦

IN MY ROOM, I wrap myself in my bedsheets. It's a poor approximation of Violet's room, but it does make me feel a little better. Muffled voices rise from the floor like steam, but I do my best not to listen. I'm thankful when the heating vent above shudders to life and blows warm air on me in rasps.

I look at the empty floor where shattered glass had been earlier. My mom must have cleaned it up when she was looking for me. She was thorough. Even as the waning light wafts in my window, I see no sparkle to indicate a speck she may have missed. Only the streaks of purple that stain the hardwood, a hue of bruise that looks like blood from a ten-year murder.

I want to cut.

I run my nails up my scars, but they are too dull to damage. I dig deeper, trying uselessly to scratch the itch of my addiction to pain. As I do, I hear Violet's voice in my head. *Life will hurt enough without you hurting yourself. I do hope one day you're able to stop.* I can almost hear the words in my ears, as if she whispers them to me from feet away. I glance at the wall in the hope that they had been muted by the plaster, but there is no sign of Violet, an opening, or anything other than this little bedroom in this little house in a little town in the forest.

I force myself to relax my grip on my forearm, my feelings floundering at the absence of an edge. I take a deep breath, thinking of the cigarettes my mom used to puff. When I was barely old enough to talk, she swore she would stop, and she did. For me to stop cutting, that had to be possible then. If not for myself, then at least for Violet.

Violet.

I want badly to go back. But without cutting, I have no idea how to get into the wall.

I pull out my phone instead, flicking through the few feeds I follow on Facebook. On social media, I'm a leave-no-trace camper. The contract formed at friending means nothing to me. I don't interact, just take in others' opinions and make my judgments silently. That way no one can argue, no one can tell me I'm wrong but myself.

If I wanted to talk to anyone, I suppose I'd give them my number. They could text me, and maybe I would actually respond. Of course, I can't remember the last time I got a text from someone besides Mom. When I try to make a list of friends who have my number, I come up empty. Isolation is a prison I built.

In any case, swiping down the scroll of selfies calms my urge to harm. If my feed is any indication, the few friends I had in the city are doing spectacularly. Better than I am, anyway. I'm sure none of them have befriended a girl who lives in their walls, whose reality is up for debate. What would happen if I took a selfie with Violet and shared it with the world? Would it show both our smiling faces? Or would it just be a picture of me, smiling like a fuckhead, clueless to my own craziness?

I push the thought out of my head and attempt to lose myself in the scroll. It works for ten minutes before I tire of it. Putting down my phone, I cross my arms and hold my elbows. Without distraction, the urge to cut is creeping back, crawling into my ears like insects. I scratch at them before picking up my phone again. I reopen the feed a second before flipping over to my browser.

The search bar taunts me.

It's empty, like me. Empty was always my M.O. As far as anyone else was concerned, I could be replaced by an android, and no one would notice. I'm frugal with phrases, and I spend most of my time alone. The few times I had been invited to the birthdays of my peers, I either declined or arrived glumly only to depart fifteen minutes later. Suffice to say, no one knows me, least of all myself. But earlier, with

Violet, I had felt something growing in the pit of my stomach, as if I had swallowed a seed that was just beginning to sprout. Something that made me feel less empty, less of an unknown. Something that screamed to be given a name, to be cared for and protected, and, when it's grown, to be shown off to the world.

I click on the empty bar, and the keyboard pops up.

boy girl

Search.

I scroll a moment, seeing a few pages for baby names, the local Boys & Girls Club chapter. I click on the bar again, backspacing the fluke. I think for a moment before remembering a term I had heard on the internet.

ladyboy

Search.

I scroll down the results. The first entry is *Urban Dictionary*, ready and raring with a definition that seems simultaneously insulting and misguided. Further down, I'm met with articles featuring titles that make me squirm. "My Date with a Ladyboy." "10 Ways to Spot a Ladyboy." Stories of men who had been made in Thailand, eager to show off their worldliness. Two lines into the first article, I see nothing except the sharpened rantings of a fuckboy. I close it and scroll down. *Wikipedia*. I click on the link, knowing that at the very least I'll get something textbook.

"Kathoey," the article title reads, "Kathoey or katoey is a male-to-female transgender person or a person of a third gender...."

That's a new one. Quickly, I hit back to return to the search bar.

transgender

Search.

I almost scroll past the paid advertisement before the

words catch me. A poorly formatted local advert screams for my attention.

GAY ALL-DAY YOUTH GATHERING FOR LGBTQ+ KIDS & TEENS, the link reads. I click through.

I'm brought to a landing page for the Evergreen Community Center, the local non-profit I had passed on my walk back from school this morning.

Gay All Day is an after-school program for kids and teens ages 10-17. We welcome everyone, whether you are gay, lesbian, bisexual, transgender, queer or questioning. We are here to support you on your journey as you discover the truest you you can be. Our group meets on Wednesdays at 4 pm at the Evergreen Community Center.

Wednesday. Tomorrow. I could go, but I'd have to force another excuse. Since I'm on thin ice already, the prospect of pressing my luck makes me sweat. Sure, I could confess my concerns, but, well, I don't even know anything yet. I mean, do these feelings even mean anything? Maybe, like I'm told, it will pass.

I return to the search bar, intent on casting my cares on the gods of the internet.

am I transgender

Search.

The results show me a few articles, both by magazines and medical professionals, as well as a few quizzes by pop media sites. Too scared to take the latter, I click on one of the articles addressing my question, skimming through the introduction until a sentence stops me in my tracks.

"…if someone is even asking themselves this question," the article says, "it probably means, at the very least, they are not *cisgender* (i.e. they do not feel that their assigned gender at birth matches their actual gender identity)."

I exit out of the browser and drop my phone, which now

weighs a hundred pounds. Nonetheless, my heads floats off my shoulders like a balloon. I know now, I knew as soon as I began this search, that I must be something other than what I was told I was. Whatever I am, it's not what I thought. It's some kind of plot twist. I slump into my covers, the lightness giving way to the dread of what this means for me.

Will my life change? Will this hurt? What can I even do to be more myself?

My mind races through a million questions I finally have the words for. I need help, that much is certain. Help outside these walls. I open my calendar and type in the time of the Gay All-Day meeting tomorrow, though I hardly need the reminder. If my rushing blood is any indication, I won't be thinking of anything else until I get there. I don't know what a group like this will be like. I think of church services my parents used to take me to, with their white walls and white people dressed in shades of starched beige. This group, I think, must be nothing like that.

I rub my belly. The sprout in my stomach seems to grow, its leaves tickling my insides pleasantly. It feels good to fertilize myself. Up til now, I'd been overpruned. Picked down to the stem out of the fear of what would grow if you let it. I'd gotten so used to the feel of phantom flowers, that empty air where a blossom could be, that I'd started to see myself as a weed. Thrown away at the slightest sign of new growth.

But weeds are just plants in the wrong place. Enigmas society doesn't know what to do with. Maybe there will be people like me at the meeting tomorrow, other weeds that have been cut down or thrown away. Other flowers spayed before they could sprout. Will I belong? Will this be the "right place" for someone like me to grow? Will I even be able to grow, or am I really as broken as I feel?

Tomorrow is budding with promise. I want tomorrow to be

now. I want to go to the meeting, and ask my questions before they break out of me. I want to tell Violet about my discovery, but I have no way to reach her. Even though it's early, I tuck myself into bed and squeeze my eyes shut. The morning can't come soon enough.

9

This morning I told my mom that there was a mandatory pep rally after school, that I would need to be picked up later than usual. Since she had been called about my skipping class, her trust in me is depleted. She peppered me with questions like a zealous cook seasoning a dish with the ideal pinch of guilt. Luckily, I had answers prepared. It was the beginning-of-the-year rally, of course. The time when the staff gathers the students together to elucidate the school's goals for the upcoming year. This year, I lied, Maple Middle wanted to build a new field, and to do so would require the planning of a handful of fundraising events, the first of which would be determined tonight. My mom had remained quiet for a moment, probing my story for holes. I continued to say that I regretted skipping class before, and I wanted this rally to mark a renewed commitment to being the best student I can be at Maple Middle. I had even made a potential new friend, I told her, smiling a little. Him and I were supposed to sit together at the rally. His name was Charlie, and he liked to draw pictures of superheroes and robots.

Though the details were a tad overwrought, she swallowed

them with a cough. She even told me she was proud of me for stepping up, and that she hoped I had a good time. When I smiled in response, the seed that grew the day before turned a stone in my gut.

I gritted through the school day, fending off interaction with my signature aloofness until the final bell rang.

I walk to the strip mall a few blocks from Maple Middle. The fall sun shines over the small collection of stores that comprise the town's only shopping center. In the warm light, every blemish is visible. Cracks crawl through concrete, and the glass storefronts are finger-smeared and painted with a dirty beige film. Few of the signs are intact, and those that flicker sickly. I read *Evergreen Auto Insurance* in bold blue letters cracked open to reveal their innards. The local Chinese restaurant has attempted to hide their shame with cardboard, though now their sign reads only *Chin.* I scan for my destination, the store I had spent lunch scrolling for under the table. I finally find it, poised coyly on the far end of the strip. The light-up letters have been removed, leaving only the outline of the store's name traced in years of stain. *Sylvie's Secondhand,* it reads.

I stuff my hand inside my pocket, feeling for the five-dollar bill I had saved instead of buying lunch. Satisfied that I will be able pay my way to gay, I take a deep breath and walk in the store.

The glass door creaks open, tapping a bell that sounds fuller than it should for its size. I hear a rustling in the back of the empty store, and a gray-haired woman emerges from the overfull racks of used couture. She looks a little startled by me, as if she was not actually expecting customers today.

"Hello, young man," she says. "You know, we don't have many things in here that boys your age would like, though I think I may have acquired a skateboard earlier this week."

As she talks, she weaves her way to the checkout counter, a glass rectangle chock full of odds, and leans over it. A collection of bright beaded necklaces falls from her blouse and clatters onto the counter.

"It's missing a wheel," she tells me, as if that somehow sweetens the deal.

"Oh," I say. "No thank you. I'm actually looking for something else."

I had spent the majority of my classes locked in my head, reciting the story I hoped would fend off suspicion. I imagined, after all, that few teenage boys came into *Sylvie's* to buy themselves a dress.

"Okay," the woman says, looking confusedly around her wares. "How can I help you?"

"Tomorrow is my sister's birthday," I tell her. "My twin sister."

"Well, happy birthday!" the woman says. "What are you thinking of getting her?"

It takes me longer than I would like to admit to realize that if tomorrow was my nonexistent twin's birthday, it must be mine, too. A minor detail that I had completely flubbed in the preparation of my alibi.

"Thank you," I stutter, "and I'm not quite sure. She likes dresses."

The woman rises from the glass counter amid the clatter of beads.

"Well then. Follow me."

She vanishes into the racks of old fabric, and I follow her. I feel like I am foraging through a foreign land, a world I had never know existed. I half-expect Violet to be waiting for me somewhere inside the mecca of used clothing, waiting patiently to help me procure the perfect piece. My heart thumps with the fear that I will be found out, and my hands shake in my pockets.

"Our dresses are over here," the woman motions to a rack wrung with curtains of colorful fabric.

"She's the same size as me," I blurt. A necessary detail I am over-eager to share.

The woman looks me up and down. If she's suspicious, she doesn't show.

"I'd guess small, maybe medium." She begins flicking through the dresses. "Do you know what color she likes?"

"Purple, especially dark purple," I tell her, adding, "I think."

Performative uncertainty is key in this situation, or that's what I tell myself. I'm smart enough to know that a bold-faced lie can be seen through like glass.

We stand silent for a moment amid the screeking of hangers against the bar.

"Are you Sylvie?"

My amateur attempt at being personable.

The woman laughs, shakes her head.

"No. I'm her daughter. My mom started the store back in the seventies. Back then, it was a way for poorer families to find cheap clothes. Church project."

I tune out.

The word *church* hits like a brick, a reminder of where I reside, how vital it is that I keep who I am to myself. When I was younger, my parents had taken me to a church in the suburbs of the city. I was unloaded into a room that smelled like piss and fish crackers, given a small tome that read *The Gospels*. The other kids, a collection of *nouveaux riche* specimens, seemed too preoccupied with the snacks and games to give much thought to what the adults in the room were telling us. They told us a story they called a *parable*. A story about seeds and soil, about when and how the seeds grow. When it was over, they asked us what kind of trees we would grow into if we were seeds. *A pear tree,* one girl said. *We have one in our backyard and it's yummy!* A blunt-haired boy raised his hand and shouted *A gun tree!* without asking permission to speak. I was the last in the circle. When they got to me, I said *I don't care what kind of fruit I have, but I want to be a girl tree.* The other kids laughed, and the adults looked stern for a moment before telling me that I must have misunderstood the question. *Apples* was all I said after that. From then on, I made every excuse I could think of not to go back, and eventually my parents stopped going altogether.

Screeeek.

The woman who is not Sylvie pulls a purple dress from the rack and hands it to me.

"Do you think she'd like this?"

I hold it up to examine, careful to be clear that I am not holding it up to my body to size myself for it. I can't seem too eager. The dress looks like something you would buy at a costume store. Princess purple satin shines in the fluorescent light. The bodice is traced with gold lace, and the skirt billows atop a cloud of crinoline. I can't help but turn up my nose.

"I don't think so. It's a little extravagant. I'm looking for something more casual," I say, adding, "for my sister."

The woman who is not Sylvie gives me a skeptical look and retrieves the dress from my hand. She squeaks through a few more before pulling another off the rack.

"How about this?" she holds it up.

The dress is a simple shade of purple that's obviously been well-washed in its lifetime. A faded hue and balls of lint show its age, and, I hope, its comfort. The V-shaped neckline is accented by a few crisscrossed straps to distinguish it as more than just a tee. It looks perfect, like something I would find in

Violet's closet. The woman slides her hand into the seam of the skirt.

"And it has pockets!" she says.

I have to clench my fist to keep myself from snatching the garment from her.

"She loves pockets!" I respond, trying my best to hide my excitement. "How much?"

The woman checks the tag.

"Seven-fifty," she says, then smiles. "But for such a nice brother, I'll give it to you for five."

"I'll take it!" I say, disbelieving my luck.

She leads the way back to the glass counter, lays it on top while I fish out my five dollars. She takes the bill and folds it into the ancient cash register to her right.

"Tell your sis happy birthday for me," she says as she arranges the pittance of profit.

"Will do! Thanks again!"

The woman shoots me one last look of skepticism as I grab the dress and stuff it in my bag, nearly running for the door. I don't breathe steadily until the echo of the bell dissipates into the autumn air. All I can think of as I make my way to the community center is how soft the fabric felt as I put my first dress in my backpack, and how soft it'll feel on me.

10

I panic as soon as I enter Evergreen Community Center.

This step is scary. If this were war, I would be the forbidden child crossing enemy lines. It feels dangerous to be here, as if at any moment I could be stopped with spotlights and cuffed for my crimes. I still haven't said it, not out loud, but the fact that I'm attending tonight is me admitting for the first time outside my head that the doctor made a mistake when they told my parents *It's a boy.*

Ahead, the only open door in the place yawns fluorescently, while inside a copse of kids around my age chat each other up. In most situations with children, the wall between boy and girl is built high and thick. Stay to your side, or else risk lifelong exclusion. But even from across the hall, I can see that no such structure exists here. There are as many representations of what a person can be as there are people in the room, and they're all beautiful in their own way. I find myself excited to graft myself into a group of strangers for maybe the first time in my life.

My dress.

I want to put it on, to arrive wearing myself on my sleeve.

Two dark blue doors interrupt the wall to my right, one reading *Men* and one *Women*. As I walk up to them, the oldest of the people from the group heads for them as well. A tall woman, with long brown hair and a heavy brow. She appears older than the age range the group is geared towards, so I assume she must be a facilitator. She smiles at me, a smile full of joy and free of judgment.

"Hello," she says casually.

Her voice is like dark honey, and it echoes in my ears as she pushes open the door marked *Women* and vanishes inside.

I realize that it was instinct that brought me here, like a lost crow drawn over distance to find its murder.

She's like me.

I look between the two doors before me, racking my brain for the answer no one can give me. The woman had just walked into the restroom liked she belonged there, and it takes me a moment to realize that's exactly the case. My mind fumbles to rebuild the binary she had so simply toppled, only to form a something pathetic and laughable. If I wasn't fear-frozen in the face of it, I might have the urge to jibe this binary for the joke that it is.

As I make my way for the women's room, something pricks at me. A burning on the back of my neck as if the world is watching me, my family in the forefront. In my head, they look at me with a cocktail of derision and concern.

What the hell *do you think you're doing, young man?*

My father's voice bounces off the brick, each echo boxing my ears with the shame of what I'm becoming.

I glance around hastily then slip through the door marked *Men*. Deciding on this door is defeat, though I can't conclude what battle I've lost. Luckily, the bathroom is empty, and I creep into the one stall past the urinals and lock it behind me. Unzipping my backpack, I pull out the purple dress I had so proudly purchased. I shake off my old clothes and find myself stopping every second to listen for footsteps. At any moment, someone could burst in and I'd be found out. It feels like somewhere out there is a Protestant paparazzi dead-set on discovering my shame, and soon their lenses will surface beneath the stall walls and scar me for life.

When I finally get the dress on, I quickly zip up my pack and listen to the silence once more before sprinting to the door. The mirror's magnetism begs me to see how I look in this new thing, but terror drives me into the hallway prematurely.

I emerge from the men's room with so much speed the door slams behind me. A few feet away, the woman from minutes ago walks toward the open door at the end of the hall. She turns around as if startled by the sound.

I squeeze my eyes shut, trying to block out the embarrassment. The woman only smiles again, a secret smile of knowing.

"I love that dress!" she says. Then, pointing to the open door, "Are you gonna join us?"

I nod and let her lead me into the room. The rest of the group stares at me only a moment before returning to their conversations.

"I believe this seat's free," the woman tells me, guiding me to one of the many open chairs set up in a circle.

I sit, and she walks a few chairs over and takes a seat as well. She flutters her hands together in a clattery clap and clears her throat.

"Is everybody ready to start?" she asks no one in particular.

A few standers bumble to nearby seats, and those who were conversing hush when they hear her speak. These kids, they respect her, in a way I have never seen someone my age respect an adult before. As if her honesty about who she is has formed an honest bond. The woman looks around the room, peering through thick glasses to make smiling contact with each person before she continues.

"Wonderful," she says. "Is it anyone's first time here?"

Her gaze falls on me as she says it. My hand is the only one to raise, and the group's attention falls on me. My shivering intensifies as I feel the air get colder.

"Thank you for joining us," the woman says. "Do you mind if we introduce ourselves first, and then you can tell us who you are?"

I nod, relieved that I will not be put on display.

"Aria," the woman says to a teenage girl on her right, "would you like to start? Name, pronouns, and, um, let's see. Favorite dinner food."

The lean teenager sits tall in her chair, her mouth eagerly open to let the words out. My heart flutters a little. Her dark, willowy hair, the way her eyelashes land on her cheeks like butterflies make my stomach buzz. I do my best not to stare.

"I'm Aria," she says, giggling. "Which she already said. My pronouns are she/her/hers, and my favorite dinner food is sushi."

When the girl says the last word, her eyes flit to around the circle and land on me. She smiles, and my cheeks fill with blood. I rub them, hoping it doesn't show.

"Thank you, Aria," the woman says. "Next?"

To Aria's left, a boyish kid spouts up, bouncing up and down on the front wheels of a wheelchair.

"Hey, I'm Asher. He/him/his. Ze/zir if ya nasty." Asher chuckles to himself. "Uh, I really like mac'n'cheese, like the blue box shit."

"So good!" Aria says.

The woman chuckles.

"Okay, next person."

A few empty chairs to the left of Asher, a tree of a kid grows out of the beige plastic chair. Green hair sprouts from their head in worm-like dreadlocks, and their dark eyes are precisely lined to catty points. They slump back as they begin to speak, as if the words wear them down.

"My name is Krystyn. I'm nonbinary, they/them/their pronouns." I close my eyes and soak up their tone, rich with soft confidence that defies their meek posture. "I'm vegan, and my favorite thing to eat for dinner is Chipotle's sofritas."

Their eyes glaze with the memory of the meal.

"Thank you Krystyn," the woman says. "I love your eyeliner, by the way!"

"Thanks," they whisper.

"Okay," the woman continues, making eye contact with me, next in the circle. "We'll come back to you in a second. Nathan?"

To my left sits a small figure, bushy hair grown medium-long and wire-framed glasses. They clear their throat before speaking.

"I'm Nathan," the kid says, tugging on their skirt. "I'm not really sure of my pronouns yet, so you can use they/them for now. Um, I'm not a big food person, but I really like instant ramen with peanut butter."

"Ewwww!" Aria says, giggling.

Nathan rolls their eyes.

"It's actually really good," they say. "You should try it."

"Okay, my turn," the woman interjects. "My name is Suzanne, and my pronouns are she/her/hers and sometimes they/them/theirs. As many of you know, I absolutely *love* tacos, especially carnitas!"

A chorus of yums erupts around the room. Suzanne chuckles and then turns to me.

"Do you want to go now? Your name, pronouns, and favorite dinner food?"

My cheeks flush as I start to speak.

"Oh, uh, yeah, sure."

Aria giggles, shooting me a playful look as I stumble through my words.

"Um, this is my first time here, or anywhere like this," I say. "Sorry if I mess it up."

"I don't think you could," Suzanne tells me. "Please share whatever you're comfortable with and thank you for being brave enough to show up!"

I swallow and my spit tastes like lukewarm tea. I've never been called brave before. I was the kid called *pussy* for my fear of the physical, but as Suzanne says it I realize that it is brave of me to be here. This is new territory, not just for me, but for everyone I've ever met. I feel like a pioneer into new lands of social exploration. By refusing to squelch it all, I'm building a new type of person for a new type of world.

"I guess, I don't really know what my name is."

I wince and glance around, waiting for the hammer of judgment to drop. The other kids just sit silently, smiling and ready to listen.

"At least, not yet." I continue. "For now, you can call me Bug. It's a nickname."

"Well, that's perfectly normal," Suzanne replies. "For a lot of us, it took time to find our names, our real names. If you're new to this, it makes sense that you're unsure. Do you have pronouns you like to go by?"

I scrunch my face for a moment before diving into the deep end.

"She/her/hers," I tell the group. "I'm not sure exactly what's going on with me, but I definitely feel like I might be a girl."

"You know," Suzanne says. "You just might. Those feelings don't come for no reason. So, Bug, what do you like to eat?"

I ponder the question. To date, food had been fuel and nothing more. I did my best to consume what was put in front of me, but like every other facet of my life, it was not something I found joy in. I think through the meals I've had over the past few months, searching for anything that stands out.

"I'm not sure," I say. "When I was a kid, I really liked bean burritos from Taco Bell."

"Mmm," Aria says. "Crunchwrap Supreme."

The group laughs, and Asher makes slurping noises.

"Gotta love it," Suzanne says. "Well, Bug thank you so much for being here and sharing a little about yourself. I hope you come to learn that this is a safe place for you to explore who you are and who you want to be."

I nod and do my best to smile through shaky lips.

"Now!" Suzanne exclaims. "Like I said last week, today I was planning on talking about bathrooms. Can anyone tell me why it's important that there is one bathroom for men and one for women?"

I look at Suzanne a little shocked at the question, before catching a glint of mischief in her eye.

Aria raises her hand, shouting, "It's not!"

"Gender is a construct!!" Asher spouts.

"Fuck the binary!" says Krystyn, laughing.

The rest of us burst into laughter at the joke we've been told by society. I sit back in my chair, my body relaxing for what feels like the first time. It's comfortable here. Whatever lies outside these doors, at least the group of us seem to have each other's backs.

"Does anyone else want to share before we wrap up?"

I had sat rapt during the hour or so of conversation. I had never heard anyone, let alone anyone my age, speak so freely about their desires, their will for their life. After Suzanne had properly butchered the concept of gendered bathrooms, she had gone on to ask the group where we felt most comfortable being ourselves, and how we could manifest that space in our daily lives. Aria had spoken about her grandmother, how she supported her transition despite the fact that her parents didn't. She told us the story of the first time she put on lipstick, right after she told her grandmother who she was.

Krystyn had told us about the place in the woods they liked to go to get away from everything, to escape the pressure to bend to the binary. As they described the place, I realized it must be somewhere in the woods behind my house. I mentioned that, and they said they would show me sometime. Already, I felt like I was making friends with these people. Asher's story had been short, but he talked about how he often snuck into his dad's home office, where he displayed a collection of baseball memorabilia from the past twenty years. Nathan had simply said they were not sure yet, and everyone agreed that that was okay.

Now, with unexpected eagerness, I raise my hand.

"I'll go!"

The words flit from my mouth like a butterfly.

"Sure, Bug," Suzanne says. "Where do you feel the most comfortable to be yourself?"

"Uh," I say.

I dig through the folds of my brain for a cover story, something that seems less crazy than Violet and her room in the walls. Disarmed as I am in this space, I come up with nothing. I take a deep breath and jump into the cold waves of truth below.

"Okay. This might sound a little crazy. I'm still not sure what it all means."

"This is a judgment-free zone," Suzanne tells me. "No one is going to call you crazy. No one will think any less of you. And you don't have to know what it means yet. That's why we're here. To explore."

As she speaks, she glances around the group and elicits nods from the other kids. It calms my fears a little, but I still shake as I start speaking.

"I cut myself," I say. "I *used to* cut myself. I don't anymore."

Suzanne smiles at me.

I continue, "Anyway, the last few times I cut myself, something weird happened. It's like, when I sliced my skin open, I also opened a hole in one of the walls in my bedroom. And when I did, I realized there was someone inside." I pause, flinching. "Um, anyway, I was scared she was stuck somehow, so I cut myself more to let her out. But we talked for a bit, and she told me she actually lives in the wall, like some sort of house fairy or something." I hear a giggle but push on. "We kinda got along. It was like I made a new friend, which doesn't really happen for me."

I look around the circle of chairs, bracing for bad looks, but everyone seems to be listening intently. They're trying to understand, even if they're a little confused. I keep going before the words puke out of me.

"I'm kinda skipping over a lot, but, so, the next time I cut myself the same thing happened. The girl in the walls came out and said hi. Only this time she invited me to where she lives, and I followed her. Her room was really cool. It was like dark and cozy, but also girly, and she had a lot of cool clothes, and cats, and we just talked and watched TV and she helped me with makeup and stuff."

I pause and take a deep breath. I don't know if I've said

that many words at one time in my life, but the pit in my stomach feels lighter, as if I had vomited out something nasty I'd been keeping in.

"So, that's the only place I can be myself so far," I say. Then I add, "This place is really, cool, too. I wanna come back."

I stop and slump into my seat. Everyone stays silent for a moment before Suzanne speaks.

"Thank you for sharing, Bug," she says. "I'm glad you have that place, and I hope you are able to find more places like it in the near future."

By the way she looks at me, I think she thinks I am speaking in metaphor, that what I just told them was a fictional representation of a place in my head. I want to say that this really happened, really is happening, but I decide not to press my luck. I worry that Suzanne will want to talk to my parents. Then they'll know I came here without telling them, and that will be a whole thing.

Suzanne checks her pink Minnie Mouse watch.

"I think that's all the time we have for tonight," she says. "I'm sure most of your parents are here."

"Bye!" Asher shouts as he speeds out of the room. "Nice to meet you, Bug!"

Krystyn and Nathan smile at me before walking out to the entryway of the community center to wait.

Aria stands up and makes her way toward me. I gulp.

"Hey, Bug," she says. "I'm glad you came. It was nice to meet you."

Her smile spikes my bloodstream and makes my heart beat faster.

"Nice to meet you, too," I say.

"My grandma's here, so I have to go, but I just wanted to say that if you ever want a friend to help you with makeup or whatever or just hang out, you can totally come over sometime," she tells me, adding, "I know you have the girl in the walls, but, you know, if you want another place you can be yourself. My grandma is super supportive."

My eyes get hot. In the city, no one invited to hang out, even the kids I sometimes talked to at school. This immediate show of acceptance pulls at my gut. I smile at Aria.

"I'd really like that," I tell her. "Like, a lot."

I blush, hoping she doesn't suspect my obvious crush.

We exchange numbers, and she waves as she walks out of the room. As soon as she does, Suzanne steps up to me.

"I'm glad you came," she says. "And I'm glad you're making friends. If you want to come back soon, the group is having a queer variety show on Friday. Um, let's see."

Suzanne ruffles through a stack of papers she carries, flourishing a neon pink page and handing it to me. I take it, reading the words printed cheaply in a font that looks like a child drew the letters. GAY ALL DAY KIDS & TEENS FALL DRAG & VARIETY SHOW, it reads, EVERGREEN COMMUNITY CENTER, SEPTEMBER 20 @ 7PM. Beneath the title, there is a black and white photo of someone around my age smiling in layers of makeup and a trashbag dress. Unlike most people in flyers, the teen queen looks legitimately ecstatic to be on the page.

"Is that Krystyn?" I ask.

Suzanne nods.

"Their drag name is Chick 'N Tender," she laughs. "The whole thing's a ton of fun, and it's very low pressure. You can just watch if you want."

"It looks fun," I tell her. "I'd like to come, but I'm not sure if I'll be able to."

"Keep the flyer in case," she says. "Anyway, I need to lock up, but do you need to use the bathroom before we go?"

Her eyes flit to my dress. I gather that she must have been

here, too, sneaking towards the truth in secret in the only safe spaces you can find.

I nod.

"Yeah, I probably should."

Suzanne guides me into the hallway, turning to lock the meeting room door behind us.

"I can wait out here, if you'd like."

"That would be great, thank you," I say.

I step toward the blue door marked *Men.*

"You know," the echo of Suzanne's voice in the empty hall stops me. "You don't have to do that if you don't want to. This is a safe space. You can use whichever bathroom you feel most comfortable in."

I pause in front of the door. Taking a deep breath, I turn and plunge into the women's bathroom. I'm shocked by how similar it is. I don't know what I was expecting, but this room could be a photocopy of the men's room minus the urinals. Their similarity underlines the uselessness of separate spaces. My whole life, I had thought of the women's restroom as a place of mystery, a place where the secrets of gender are kept under lock and key. As I walk into the closest stall, though, I realize that I couldn't have been more wrong.

I shirk off my dress and pull on what I was wearing before. Changing into them feels like changing into wet clothes at the beach. It's your only choice, but the discomfort of it distracts you from almost anything else. I stuff the dress into my backpack then scrunch in the pink flyer before zipping it closed and walking out of the bathroom.

Suzanne greets me with a question.

"Do you need a ride home?"

I check my phone. It's close to five, but even though it's fall the sun should stay up for at least the twenty minutes it'll take me to walk back to Maple Middle and call my mom. A ride would be nice, but I don't want to risk the chance that my mom is already waiting in the parking lot. If she saw me walking, I could explain my way out of it, but if she saw me getting out of a stranger's car, I'd have to explain more than I want to.

"No, thank you," I say. "I can walk from here."

"Suit yourself," Suzanne says.

We walk out of Evergreen Community Center, and Suzanne and I say our goodbyes as she locks the glass front doors. I thank her for making me feel so comfortable, then turn and head back to Maple Middle.

As I walk, I inhale the crisp evening air. The world seems fresh and full of possibility. For the first time, I can picture a future for myself that doesn't outright suck. I close my eyes as I let the crunching of the leaves on the sidewalk soothe me.

WHEN I GET BACK to the school, I'm relieved to see that my mom's van isn't there yet. I send her a quick text telling her I need a ride, and she tells me she'll be here in five minutes.

The sky darkens as she pulls into the drop-off area with the lights on. I open the door and get in.

My mother looks around the empty parking lot.

"Everyone left already?" she asks.

I can hear the suspicion in her voice.

"Oh, yeah," I say. "Charlie had to wait around for his dad, so I waited with him and we did reading homework."

She mulls over my story.

"Then where's Charlie? I'd like to meet him."

"His dad just picked him up," I lie. "You missed him."

My mom's only response is to clonk the stick into drive and putter out of the parking lot. Her expression softens as we pull onto the empty road home.

"Did you have fun?"

I nod.

"Yeah, I was surprised but I kinda did. I'm really excited for this next year. I think it could be the best year of my life."

My mom smiles, her joy at my words overtaking any lingering suspicion.

I smile, too, knowing that the last bit, at least, was not a lie.

11

Our van crunches into the driveway as the sun drops behind of trees that tower over our house, shadows of monsters.

"Go clean up," my mom tells me. "I'll get working on dinner. Your father should be home any minute."

I respond by eagerly opening the passenger door and jumping down onto the gravel. My backpack bounces as I jog to the front door, unlock it, and pull it open. After stepping outside my circle of safety, I'm slaked for alone time, so I rush up the stairs toward my bedroom.

My mother's tone stops me halfway up.

"Vernon, what's this?"

I turn to look back, keeping my feet firm to the stairs. I choke on my heart as she flutters the flyer Suzanne had given me. As she waits for an answer, she examines it with the interest and awe of an archeologist viewing an artifact from a dead civilization.

"And where did you get it?" she follows up. "A *drag* show?"

She speaks the word like it's another language, her tongue disgusted by the taste of it.

My brain races through possible explanations, but I am too overwhelmed to come up with anything coherent.

"Nothing," is all I say. "Found it."

Without waiting for any acknowledgment, I race up the rest of the stairs and slam my bedroom door behind me, quick as if I were being chased by a ghost. I stand with my back pressed against it for minutes, wincing at the silence I expect to be broken by the angry knocks of my mother. When I am convinced that, at least for now, she will not confront me, I slump off my backpack. It clunks on the floor, heavy with my secrets. I tear off my clothing like it's on fire, ripping the button of my jeans completely away from the fabric. I slide out of them and fish my new dress out of my bag, holding my arms up and letting it slide onto my body like a sheath.

Most of the time I can work my way out of these situations. My relationship with my parents is tepid enough that they swallow any story that harbors any amount of feasibility. If they want to know the truth, they hide it well. When my mother once found me lying naked on my bed, hand on my dick, I told her only that the late summer heat was making me sweat. She didn't press.

But now, presented with the neon pink truth, she'll have to work double to ignore what she doesn't want to know.

I lean over the pieces of this mess I've made. They shimmer in my mind like the fragments of the bottle glass that had shattered on my floor what seems like ages ago. I feel the familiar pull to pain. I stand up then kneel, fishing for the box I keep under my bed. I pull it out and uncover it. My mom had cleaned up all remnants of the purple polish spill, leaving me weaponless, but I don't let that stop me. I pick up a bottle of blue and smash it on the hardwood next to me. It breaks pathetically, like a poorly cracked egg, but one large shard gleams in the pooling blue polish. I grab it thirstily.

I just want to go in the wall. I just want to see Violet.

I grip the glass between firm fingers and draw its edge from my wrist to my elbow with one firm stroke. My seams burst, and a river of red rises like tide. The burn of the cut shushes my sadness, pain plastering over all the questions I can't answer. I close my eyes, letting the warmth of my blood soothe me like showerdrops. When I open them, my vision blurs and my head floats off my shoulders like my soul's leaving. Through the fog, I see the wallpaper tear away, opening an entryway in the wall large enough for my body.

I take a shaky step into the wallspace, swaying half-conscious. I've never felt this way, never cut myself bad enough to black out, but it seems close now. Amid the dust and webs, I fall to my knees, tearing a strip of fabric from my skirt. Like Violet did, I wrap it around my forearm, tightly, putting pressure on the wound in an attempt to mother myself. My juices soak the strip, turning it from purple to violet. I grab one of the nearby studs and pull myself up, turning to look behind me. My attempt to self-heal has caused the wall to close up, the floral vines that decorate the wallpaper snaking through each other to seal the wall like I sealed my cut.

In the dark, my blurred vision turns to blindness, and I have to feel my way along the studs and around the corner towards Violet's room. In the distance, I see a line of light shining under her door. The muffled sound of sitcom infects my ears. I stumble down the hallway guided now by the smell of flowers and spice. The chatter of cats, the warmth from her room tell me I'm close. I trip forward and catch myself, using the momentum to knock on the door.

It swings open. I hear Violet gasp then feel her hands in my armpits as she hoists me to my feet.

"Bug! I wasn't expecting you."

I mumble something empty and let her lead me inside. The light from the television illuminates my view, then, just as quickly, it fades to black and I lose consciousness.

THE BLUE BLUR of the TV screen is the first thing I see. My vision is still unclear, which disorients me as I try to place myself in the fog.

"Where?" I ask the air.

I hear someone stir. Violet. I'm in Violet's room.

Footsteps followed by the creak of her bed as she sits down next to the place she must have laid me when I fell unconscious.

"Are you okay?" she asks. "You scared me, lost it and fell to the floor. Luckily you're light enough that I got you on the bed by myself."

"I think I'm okay."

The television murmurs a moment.

"Did something happen?" Violet asks. "You cut yourself, like, *really* bad."

Her words have a motherly edge.

"I'm sorry," I say. "I was just really scared."

"Did someone try to hurt you?"

"No no no," I sniff. "Um, my mom found something. I went to a queer group at the community center, and they gave me a flyer. It fell out of my bag when I got home."

"Oh," is all Violet says.

"It sounds stupid now that I say it."

"No, no. You're fine."

"It's just that," I say, "I haven't told my parents how I've been feeling. All they know is that I started cutting myself. Not that," I pause, reciting the words to myself before making them real, "I think I'm a girl."

"That makes sense," Violet says. "You're still figuring it out for yourself."

I hear the whisper of something unsaid, but I can't make it out. I ignore it.

"Did you tell her anything?" Violet asks.

I shake my head.

"No, I just ran to my room and then...came here."

I'm interrupted by Otto sauntering onto my chest. I grunt. Violet waves him away, and he runs out into the hall.

"Well," she says, "a little eyeliner makes everything better?"

My face lights up, and she smiles in response. We both know it's not true, but it's better than nothing.

"Come on, let's try a cat eye."

I push myself out of her bed. Violet puts an arm out for me to support myself as I stand up and follow her to her vanity. She flicks a switch, and the mirror light shines. The details are murky in the dim room.

How much blood did I lose?

Violet helps me onto the stool then drapes a blanket over my shoulders. She squeezes them and smiles.

"One order of eyeliner to cut a bitch," she says in a fake Southern drawl, writing on her hand like it's an order pad. "Anything else?"

I shake my head.

"That'll be it," I tell her, playing the chipper customer. "I'm stuffed."

We both laugh.

Violet digs up a black cylinder and removes the cap. It comes to a point, covered in black like a knife that was submerged in the lakes of hell. It's beautifully dangerous.

"I'm gonna need you to close your eyes and sit still," Violet says. "I'm not good at doing this on other people."

"That's okay. It's just fun to have it on."

She hums her agreement.

"Makes me feel like a girl," I say.

"Maybe that's cause you are, hun," Violet tells me. Then, "How was the group?"

Thinking about the group brightens my mood.

"It was good!" I say. "I mean, it was small but everyone there seemed really cool, like I could be friends with any of them. Like I already am."

I feel the ice-cold ink on my eyelids as Violet begins drawing. I startle a bit.

"Did you tell them how you've been feeling?"

"A little," I say. "We introduced ourselves with a name and our pronouns. I said that I thought I was girl."

"That's great!" Violet says, excitement tempered by her concentration.

I feel the point of the eyeliner trace a triangle on my outer lid.

"And I don't want to assume, but the leader and one other girl were like me," I tell her. "That was cool. Made me feel less alone."

"You mean trans?" Violet asks. "Like us?"

"Us?"

The word slips out before I can edit it. Violet had always displayed so much poise, so much confidence that I had never thought of her as anything other than a woman. *Of course she's a woman,* I remind myself, remembering something Aria said in the group. *Trans women are women.* In all the time I had been spending with Violet, I hadn't picked up on the fact that she was trans. It started to make sense that she seemed to so innately understand what I was going through.

"I mean, yeah," I say. "Like us."

Eyes still squeezed shut, I smile, hoping Violet doesn't think my remark was in poor taste. She lifts the liner, and I feel a chill on my other lid as she begins tracing the opposite eye.

I can almost hear Violet smirk.

"Yes," she says. "I'm trans, too. If you hadn't picked up on that."

I hope that I am not blushing too much.

I don't respond, but I can feel a smile forming on my face. *She said* too. Hearing someone else acknowledge what I felt I was, what I said I was, is more affirming than any epiphany I could have for myself.

"So, I'm trans," I say. Half statement, half question.

"Open," Violet says.

I do, my lids heavy with dark black ink. I blink away the blur.

Violet squeezes my shoulders and leans in as I look in the mirror.

"All I see is a woman, girl."

As she says it, I start to see it as well. The liner has accentuated my dark eyes, giving them a touch of mystery I didn't know I possessed. Violet's eyes, hovering next to mine, are also decorated with sharp points. Though my vision is still blurry, I can see clearer than I could before. In the light, we look like we could be sisters, I notice. We both have the dark eyes, the dirty hair. The way her nose crooks slightly is just like mine. If anyone were to see us together, they might even say we were twins.

Violet's expression sags with sadness, a stark difference from a second ago. I ask why with a look.

"Can I show you something?" she asks. "It's important."

"Okay," I say, flinching at the prospect of her crumbling this fantasy. "If it's important."

She walks to the glowing screen, bubbling with the excited dialogue of *Mayberry*, and she turns it so I can see.

"I've already—" I start to say, before Violet shushes me.

She looks around for a moment then pulls a remote out of the folds of her bed sheets. She clicks a button. The screen fizzes a few times before a new show comes into focus. I look quizzically at Violet, wondering what on television could be so important. She prods at the screen, and I see.

It shows my bedroom, the angle of the lens pointed slightly downward in classic sitcom style, focused on the area around my bed. On it, two boys sit facing each other, dressed fresh from a baseball game in green-stained knickers, blue-striped shirts, and navy caps emblazoned with a yellow *M*. The boys sit affectionately close, their legs almost intertwined, almost pulling each other closer. A momentary thought places this scene in a bad porno like the ones I'd found online. The thought flits away as I'm shocked to recognize the smaller of the boys.

That's me.

It's me, and it's not. I had never played sports, nor had I ever clung to such a clean appearance as the boy on screen. With his cropped hair, slim figure, and warm brown eyes, he's the type that gays would call a *twink* and straights would refer to as *a nice boy*. The way the boy on-screen holds himself is foreign to me.

The TV version of me smiles at the larger boy, who I recognize. *Beef boy.* He is dark-haired and muscle-wrought with the hint of shadow on his chin. My pulse quickens as the dark-haired boy wraps a large hand around TV me's neck and pulls him in for a tender kiss. TV me struggles momentarily, then relents, returning the kiss with the vigor of the repressed. The boys pull each other closer, their cocks visibly growing down the legs of their tight trousers.

I feel confused inside. On one hand, the boy on the TV is handsome, I realize, and I would have no qualms to him kissing me like that. But, this version of me, it's not me at all. It's me put through a strainer, me without the meat. I'm reminded of a young Mr. Hofstedter, even, timid, in hiding, and afraid.

On the screen, my bedroom door bursts open, and my mother walks in. She blushes as she sees the two boys kissing on the bed. The larger boy opens his eyes, seeing my mother staring in disgust. He immediately pushes the TV me away, punching him in the gut hard enough that he topples off the bed and curls into the floor. He stands up, shouting a word I don't have to hear to know.

Faggot.

Violet clicks the remote, and the screen changes.

My bedroom again, though there is only one figure in it. This is another TV version of me, though this one hits a little closer to home. This version of me looks like I do now. She wears a dress and leggings, and her eyes are lined with dark black triangles. TV me drops her bag and falls face-first on the bed, her body shaking. I hear the soft sound of sobbing escape the television speakers.

The camera pans around the room. It's different than the spartan starkness of my room reality. This room has been decorated somewhat like Violet's. The walls are plastered with a variety of bands posters, all depicting people in makeup and dark dress. Her dresser had been decorated with dried flowers in a black-painted vase. On her bed, a large pink plush bear reclines against the wall.

On screen, there is a knock on the door.

"Vernon!"

TV me sits up, startled by the sound. She glares at the closed door as if it was responsible for all of her problems.

"Vernon!" The door screams. "Are you okay?"

The camera cuts close, showing the bruises around her eyes that from a distance seemed like shadow. It scrolls down her body to her crossed arms. Dark blue marks pepper the red, linear scars that decorate them. She holds herself tightly, as if keeping her ribcage from falling open and letting it all out.

"Vernon!" my mother knocks on the door. Then, after silence, "You know, this wouldn't have happened if you didn't dress like that."

The crossed arms holding TV me's torso start to shake. Then the whole image does, fizzing out and in again to show a new scene.

In this one, my bedroom is barren except for a smattering of boxes messily hustled into a corner. On my bed, my mother sits in a black dress with her head held in her hands, eyes boring into the hardwood floor. The floor boasts a fresh mess of glass and nail polish she seems unsure if she should clean up.

"Thank you."

My father says this from the open bedroom door, where he is addressing an unseen figure outside. He turns around, walks to the edge of the bed, and sits close but not too close to my mother.

"We're going to get through this," he tells her.

She cries into a white square of cloth.

"I just wish he would have told us what was wrong," she says, her voice vibrating.

Violet clicks the remote, and the screen changes once more.

This scene shows our dining room, the camera panning

around our dinner table as my mother, my father, and I sit around it. This version of me is similar to the second. She wears a dress and a scarf, and her eyes are lined yet unmarred by injury. Her dirty blonde hair is shoulder-length and decorated by a pink cone held on by elastic. The TV mother lights candles on a cake, illuminating the family's faces with flickering flame.

"Happy tranniversary!" my television parents shout.

The TV version of me smiles, her eyes wet with joy.

Her father stands up, walks to her and puts an arm around her shoulder.

"We love you, baby girl, and we're proud of you," he says.

His expression shows his pride, though tempered by confusion. Perhaps he is still struggling to understand it all. Even so, his love for the girl on the screen is honest.

My TV mother joins my father and TV me. She wraps her arms around the two of them.

"I know it's hard," she says. "For all of us. But we love you, and we support you."

The on-screen family holds each other as the camera pans to where the candles flicker on the floral frosted cake.

We love you, Violet, the cake reads.

A last click, and the TV dies. I search for the meaning of what I just saw in the amorphous reflections on the empty screen.

"What was that?" I ask Violet.

"Think of it like all the directions your life could go from here," she tells me. "There's more I could show you, but I think I've made my point."

I struggle to understand.

"Your point?"

Violet crouches near me and looks into my eyes. In her eyes, brown like mine, I see the sadness I have always felt reflected back at me. But I also see hope, I see a will to live, to truly be, that outshines the sorrow.

"My point is," Violet says, "no matter what you do your life will go on until it doesn't. It's up to you whether you go with it."

She stands up and paces around the room, picking at this thing and that mindlessly.

"I'm not sure I—"

"Hiding who you are is not going to protect you. It's not going to smooth out the bumps, and it won't make you happy. It won't keep bad things from happening, and it won't make sure everything is good. Think of Mr. Hofstedter. He may be mildly successful. He may have a home he can go to at the end of each day. He may even get by without the beatings he may have suffered had he lived his life openly. And he may seem content, but when it comes down to it, he has to put a smile on his face knowing he's too ashamed to be honest about who he is to those around him."

I nod, wondering if I had even told Violet about Mr. Hofstedter.

"Do you think he's a woman, too?"

"I can't say that, and that's not the point." Violet pauses, breathing. I can tell this has been pent up. "Just promise me that you'll think about it. That you'll really think about who you are and how you want to live your life. That's the only way for you," she places a hand on my shoulder, "for *us* to thrive."

I understand that Violet means *us* as transwomen, but there seems to be more meaning to it, as if she is saying that if I keep myself hidden, she will cease to exist. I nod.

"I want to come out, I really do." I say. "I'm scared."

Violets takes her hand off my shoulder and stands up again. She looks lost in the memory of a previous pain.

"Of course you are," she says. "You'd be crazy not to be. In this world, people like us are beaten. We are fired from our jobs and overlooked by the system. We have to fight daily for the resources we need. We have to fight daily to exist." Violet's eyes well up, spill over. She wipes away the tears with the sleeve of her sweater. "I'm not telling you that coming out is going to make your life easier. Honestly, it probably won't, at least circumstantially. Some days, you won't even be able to leave your front door. Some days it'll just be too much to face the onslaught of looks, of laughter, of lust. You'll just want to hide inside, and sometimes that's okay. There's tomorrow to try again. But, if you do come out, what will change is that on those days you feel pretty enough, sure enough, and strong enough to walk out your front door, you're gonna do so as your complete and honest self. And that makes all the difference."

Violet stops talking, her face wet from crying. She sits down on her bed, eyes locked on the floor. For a moment, I wonder if she's forgotten all about me. Then she speaks again.

"Just promise me you'll think about it," is her refrain.

My body feels frozen to the stool. My head feels like it's floating off my shoulders again, running away from what Violet just showed me, just said. I grab it with my hands, holding it tight to my body. Now is not the time for escape. This is too important to ignore. Pushing myself up from the stool, I stumble to Violet's bed and sit next to her, placing my arm around her shoulders.

"I promise," I say.

My vision feels foggy. I can see the fabric tied around my forearm darkening. The cuts must have reopened. My body is a toothpaste tube being squeezed dry of its juices. The edges of my eyes go black.

Violet sniffs.

"Thank you," she says, as I go unconscious and fall to the floor.

12

———

Darkness, dotted with dust.

A familiar voice, full of fear, then the brief comfort of the couch.

Lilting lights, the wail of a banshee, the rapid rolling of wheels.

Bright white, a rusty tinman, and the forms of ghosts gathering.

The blue bed, hard but soft, raised like a chair amid an electronic chorus, and the curtain is drawn.

All things halfway taken.

My soul struggles to stay above the surface.

I WAKE up in a sea of blue. My arms are tied with tubes, and I feel the cold rush of saline replenishing my veins. I am dressed in a hospital gown, the irony of it not lost on me. My body is propped against the bed like a puppet, my limbs soupy from slumber. A few feet away, my mother sleeps feline in a round chair, chin on chest. Our circle has been closed, wrapped packagely in a sheet like wrinkled sky.

I open my mouth to call my mother, but instead let the beeping of the pulse monitor silence me. The dryness in my throat taste like chalk, stops me from talking, though I'm not sure I want to. The quiet quenches me.

Over my lap, a bed table is dressed with an undesirable meal, dousing my already absent appetite. A clear plastic glass sits empty beside it. I will it to water me.

As if in response, the blue curtain clinks open, and a tall woman dressed in beige leans through. She looks at my mother, then to me, and points at her sleeping form.

I shake my head.

The woman slips through the curtain and sidles up to my bedside. Her lanky limbs hang off her body like willow-branches, and a strong brow half-hides her kind green eyes.

She leans in and whispers, so as to not wake my mother.

"My name is Elle. I'm a nurse. I just came in to check on you," she says. "Do you need anything?"

Her voice is sugar and grit. It reminds me of Suzanne from the community center group.

I look at the empty cup.

"More water?"

I nod.

The nurse takes the glass and disappears through the curtain.

The way she walks is awkward but certain, as if she is confident only in how ill this world fits her. In my hazy mind, it clicks.

She's like me.

The sheet rustles and the nurse returns with a full glass of water. She brings it to my bedside, and gently pushes it to my lips. I drink it down in nearly one gulp.

"Guess I'll get more," she chuckles, vanishing again.

When she reappears, she holds two full glasses and places them on the dinner tray.

"I want you to sip these," she says. "I don't want you getting nauseous. And when your mom wakes up, I want you to have some food."

Her tone is more motherly than any I have heard, as if she took classes in soothing speech. I hear the pulse monitor slow a touch. She sits on the edge of the bed, takes my bad arm in her hands and examines the thick bandages that cover it to the elbow. Flecks of purple are still visible on my nails. I fight my instinct to hide them.

"You're going to be okay this time," she whispers. "No broken promises today, but I really hope this doesn't happen again. You're young. And believe it or not, things do turn out okay, at least enough of the time that it's worth going on." She pauses, then asks, "What should I call you?"

I nod at the clipboard clung to the edge of the bed.

Her face falls.

"I know that," she says. "But, is that what you want to be called?"

I shake my head and look nervously at my mother. She still sleeps curled into the chair.

"It's okay," the nurse assures. "Between you and me."

I take a deep breath.

"Violet," I tell her. My voice sounds like overstretched silk.

"I thought so," she says. "Like knows like. Violet is a beautiful name."

My mother stirs and I startle. She sits up in the chair, blinks loudly, and looks at the nurse and I.

Was she listening?

"Oh, hello," my mom says to the nurse. Then to me, "You're awake."

I nod.

"I just came in to fill up h—," she stumbles. "To replenish the water and check bandages. Everything is looking good."

She sets my arm down and stands. My mother looks at her incredulously.

"Thank you," she says.

Elle nods before sweeping open the curtain. She pauses.

"Please let me know if you need anything. Your kiddo is a sweetie, and I want to make sure..."

"Thank you," my mother interrupts. "We will."

Elle smiles, winks at me, and vanishes through the sheet. Her shoes squeak across the sterile tile as she leaves the room.

Mom rubs her eyes with her fists.

"How are you?" she asks me.

"Okay," I say. "Tired."

She nods.

"You should rest."

I lay back in the bed, saying nothing.

After a moment, my mom speaks again.

"I'm going to call your father and give him the update," she says. "I'll be just outside."

The pulse monitor beeps faster.

Did she hear?

"I'm gonna sleep."

My mom digs through her purse and pulls out her phone. She leaves the room like wind.

I close my eyes, trying to slow the beep of the heartrate monitor, tuning into the cold buzz of saline. I feel a bit better after the water, and I do my best to drift off.

A few minutes later, I hear the steps as my mother makes her way back into the room. I keep my eyes closed, hoping she thinks I'm asleep.

IN THE MORNING, the sun falls through the window like water, waking me. The blue curtain that had surrounded me the night before has been pulled open, and a few feet away my mother murmurs to Elle the nurse.

My sleep-addled mind makes out snippets of the conversation.

"...wanted to check in before you go. Hydration is important..."

"...I just want to know why he..."

"...take today off from school..."

"...thank you, sir, I mean, miss..."

By the time I am fully awake, Elle has left the room, and my mom paces in front of the window, her form a black ghost created by sunlight. In the chair she had slept in, there is a pile consisting of her purse and the clothes I must have come in wearing. The purple dress I had on last I was conscious is nowhere to be seen. Violet must have carried me back to my room and dressed me like a boy before I was found, as the only clothes I see are jeans and a tee.

"You awake?" my mom asks, startling me.

"Uh, yeah."

"The nurse said we can leave whenever you're ready."

I nod. I don't want to leave, not yet. As sick as I feel at the fact that I spent the night in the hospital, going home means meeting the consequences face to face. It means explaining to my parents why I did this or escaping it any way I can. It means keeping my promise. Finding myself here has been a shock. Cutting had always seemed harmless enough, just a bit of blood lost, and no real harm done. But now, I know what will happen if I take it too far.

I think of the kids in the group. They'd all been so nice to me, and they'd all seemed relatively happy to be there. To be themselves.

I wanna be like that.

I wanna be happy to be here.

I wanna be myself.

13

———

The car ride from the hospital is fifteen minutes, but the early afternoon traffic stretches it to twenty. Mom had let me sleep in late and checked me out with hardly a word. Now, as she hunches over the steering wheel, her features contort in forced concentration on the tail lights ahead.

She set me up in the back of the car, strapping me in the middle with a water bottle and a bag for the nausea. I don't have to puke, but I wish I did just so something would break the silence.

Halfway into the drive, I gather the courage to speak.

"I'm sorry," is all I say.

The empty words rattle like a penny in a can.

She doesn't know what I'm really apologizing for, and neither, I suppose, do I. For letting a bad thing get worse, maybe. For nearly bleeding dry the vessel she birthed me in. No, and no. I don't feel guilty for those things. I feel guilty for what I now know I need to tell her, the few little words that are going to wreck our relationship for years. *Mom, I'm a girl.* The phrase sticks in my throat like broken glass and I almost cough it up before I panic and choke it down again. Not yet. I'm not ready to jump off that cliff.

Instead, I let my weak apology steep in the hopes it'll become her cup of tea.

Mom says nothing, her only expression the death grip she holds the wheel with, her knuckles shining pale in the hazy autumn sun.

She says nothing for the rest of the ride. It's not until we crunch into the gravel drive that she speaks, and then only after a span of silence.

Mom turns around in the driver's seat, bracing her hand against the passenger headrest, and says one word.

"Why?"

It's my turn to be quiet.

Inside, my blood rushes through my veins, screaming to get out, to release all this pressure once and for all. I want it gone, this burning in my stomach. I want to be done with the cutting and the bleeding. I want to be done with the suffering in silence, the being called a faggot because people *think* I am instead of *know* I am. I want to rip off the old skin and show off what's underneath, even if it hurts to do so. Even if the new skin is sensitive and tender, and the softest breezes burn. At least then I would be on my way to healing, to thickening my skin to the wounds the world will give me, instead of making my own.

But I don't.

"I'm sorry," is all I say.

My mom palms her face and breathes in deep, letting the breath out in shaky spurts.

"Vernon, no one just all of the sudden tries to commit suicide."

That's not my name, I want to say, but I say nothing.

My mom looks at me with the eyes of a victim, eyes that ask in tears why I'm hurting her so. I don't know what to say.

"I'm sorry."

With another shuddery sigh, my mom reapplies her fake-nice face. She even gives me a bit of a smile.

"Let's go inside," she says. "You should lie down. We can talk later."

I CLOSE my bedroom door behind me and slide down the dirty wood. I let myself soak in the silence, let the lack of sound pull me out of reality and into my mind. As I settle into my inner world, I hear the subtle strokes of a guitar lapping at the air like the tide. I listen through the door. My parents never played music, and I'd be surprised if the sound was from them. Anyway, it doesn't sound like it's coming from downstairs. The plucked notes prick at the back of my head, and I turn around again. It's coming from in here. It's coming from inside the walls.

Violet, what do I do now?

Instinctively, I pull up my sleeve and poke at the bandage that has been professionally placed over my wounds. The sting of tender flesh nips at my nerves as I do. To get inside the wall, will I have to cut again? That's all I want to do, to run and hide forever in the spaces society forgets. But, if I do, what will happen? Will I end up, again, in a hospital bed, counting the drip-drops of the IV? If anything, the past day has proven the path self-harm would lead me down. I'd waste away until there's nothing left.

I close my eyes and let the music melt into my mind. Maybe this will have to suffice. Maybe Violet's room is my closet to come out of, and maybe it's best left closed. When choosing between being a target and being tucked away, is the latter all that shameful? Is my best move to live outside the temple I'd built, when it's so safe inside?

I picture Violet in her room, cozied up with Ottoman while the television bubbles. My skin feels warm at the thought of it. The sound of the plucked notes gets louder, and the above it a sultry voice begins to sing. I open my eyes.

The sound *is* in here. I stand up and nearly fall back again when I see that the opening in the wall yawns wide and vacant. Quickly, I examine my arm to make sure I have not sprung a stitch, but everything is in order. In any case, I feel fine. I feel better than ever, and my pulse racehorses as I take a few steps into the dusty dark.

Ahead, the corner glows with the suggestion of light beyond. I walk carefully through the cobwebs, making sure to steady myself with my unstitched arm. The music is louder now, and the familiar smell of flowers and spice invigorates my senses.

"Violet!"

I'm so excited I can't wait the length of the hallway to make myself known.

Ottoman skitters ahead before slipping through the slit of light that illuminates the crack of her door. I walk faster till I'm almost running, chasing the cat's tail until I burst into the room, panting from the exertion.

14

Violet is wrapped in a blanket on her bed, petting the purring cat as he loafs on the covers. When she hears me, she turns.

Her smile is warm, but her skin looks clammy and pale, as if she had come down with something since last I saw her.

"Are you okay?" I ask.

Her pale cheeks color blush pink, as if she's embarrassed by her own state.

"Oh, I didn't mean," I stutter. "You look fine, just sick is all."

As if to affirm my suspicions, Violet coughs hard into the crook of her arm. Ottoman raises his hackles at the offense and jumps off the bed with a thud.

"A little," Violet says, "but I'll be fine."

Her complexion tells me otherwise, but I don't push.

"Will you?" Violet asks, nodding at my bandaged arm.

I nod.

"Thanks for getting me back," I say.

Violet smiles though her expression looks tired.

"I'm just glad you're okay," she says.

I wait for her to continue, to ask me to tell her all about it, but she doesn't.

"I wanted to tell my mom," I confess.

"But you didn't?" Violet asks.

I shake my head.

"I did tell a nurse," I say. "A nurse who's like us."

Violet bobs her head excitedly.

"What did you say?" she asks, perkier than she was a minute ago.

"I told her my name," I say. "Not Vernon."

Violet stands up, swaying then steadying herself. She gives me a hug. I feel her scant weight hang from my shoulders.

"I'm so proud of you! How did it feel?"

"Good," I say. "Really good."

Violet holds me at arm's length and looks me in the eye.

"So what's the next step?"

I had come here to ask her that, but even as she asks me I realize I know.

"There's a drag night at the queer kids and teens club tonight," I tell her. "I was thinking of getting dressed up to go."

"Will you be okay?"

"I think so," I say, regarding my arm. "It doesn't hurt too bad."

"Does that mean you're going to tell them?" Violet asks, meaning my parents.

I freeze. I hadn't thought about that. Violet seems to want me to. She's almost desperate, as if my coming out is the medicine she needs.

"Maybe," I say, meaning no.

Violet's expression droops a bit, before she slathers a smile over it.

"Do you want help getting ready?" she says.

She does her best to beam, but the light inside her has dimmed.

WHEN I'M BACK on my side of the wall, I'm wearing one of Violet's flashiest dresses. Silky polyester drapes my shoulders, exposing them for the meager things they are. A knee-length skirt sprouts from my waist, and its sequins sparkle as I spin. Violet helped me with my makeup, though this time my own hands did the work. The lack of finesse is obvious, thick squiggles top each eye, and the outline of my lips is shaky. I love it nonetheless, like you love an ugly kitten because it's yours. I dodder out of the wallspace on low heels that Violet lent me, a compromise to keep me from falling off her highest highs.

Downstairs, it's quiet.

Something like speech leaks through my woodslat floor, though it's impossible to tell if it's my parents or the television.

I soft-toe to my door, hoping my awkward steps don't alert my parents to my indiscretion. I open it a crack and listen. The words are illegible, but the singsong tones tell me that my mother has tuned into the evening news. She'll be distracted, and far from the front door. Quickly, I gather up my bag and sneak out of my room and down the stairs. I hold my breath as I reach the last, making doubly sure no one is hiding around the corner. From the living room, I hear my mother sniffling over sips of what I imagine must be wine. I make for the front door like a drowning girl swimming for the surface, and only once I am outside with the door locked behind me do I allow myself to breathe the air.

It's early evening, though late in the season, and the air is nippy on my newly bare legs. I let it wake me up, let it invigorate me. The sun is halfway set, and I pray to nothing that the lack of detail it lends keeps me safe as I walk to Evergreen Community Center.

Without pause, I clomp to the end of my street and turn,

on the off chance that my mom finds an empty room and comes to search for me. I don't want them to know where I'm going, not yet. As I catch my breath on the adjacent street, I shiver. Slouching off my backpack, I pull out one of Violet's oversized flannels and wrap it around me. It helps, if only a bit.

As I reach the next turn, I hear voices.

My heart speeds, and I kick myself for thinking I could reach the community center unseen. This town is small, but not that small.

I listen to swelling conversation, summing up my opponents to the best of my ability. Their voices sound young, my age, and even the slightest bit familiar. As I pick apart the sentences, I hear one that catches my ear.

"...wouldn't fuck a jock if you paid me."

The deadpan diss is familiar, and in my mind I return to the halls of Maple Middle. It sounds like the group of goth girls that haunt the halls like shrikes. My breath eases a little. The girl who had just spoke was the one who told off that meathead for calling me a faggot. If I was to run into anyone looking like this, I suppose the hounds of Hot Topic would be the least of the evils.

I inhale hard and step around the corner with all the grace of a broken-winged bird skipping along the cement. I almost run into one of the girls as I do, tripping to the side at the last second as they pass.

I speed, before I get far I'm stopped by recognition.

"You're the new kid, right?"

It's the girl who had defended me before.

Fuck fuck fuck.

Part of me wants to start running, but I know that would only make this worse. I turn around to face the gaggle of goths. As I do, they giggle a bit. I feel myself flush, and I hope my foundation covers up my embarrassment. I don't feel ready for this, but then I suppose you never do.

"Oh, uh, yeah," I say. "Hi."

The uneasy depth of my voice makes me suddenly self-conscious, and I wrap the flannel tighter to try and hide my truth.

The girl who had spoken looks me up and down with an expression that tells me she doesn't know what to make of this. I imagine what a clown I must look right now. At school, I was known for nothing besides being the target of teasing, and now I'm proving every word of it true.

Fag-got, fag-got.

"How's it going?" she stumbles over the words, her regret for starting the conversation obvious. "Uh, what's your name again?"

My mind races through the options. If I tell her my real name, I risk the school knowing what I am. If I don't I risk them thinking I'm something else entirely. I swallow a chunk of air and choke on it, coughing a moment before I can speak.

"Oh, uh," I trip. "Ver-ver, Violet."

I'm met by a collection of blank stares. One of the girls starts to laugh until the girl I was talking to shushes her.

"I'm Roni," she tells me, walking up to me. She shakes my hand as she says, "Nice dress."

"Thanks," I force out.

Roni looks back at her black-clad clan.

"Anyway," she says. "I'll, uh, see you around."

I say nothing, only nodding in response as I watch Roni rejoin her group and walk away. For a moment, I think every-thing might be okay, but as they rounds the corner and retreat from view, the cackling starts. In my head it sounds like hyenas, a predatory pleasure that makes me feel alone and in danger. I stand in the cold as the light loses a few shades, shivering in my sequin dress.

I can't.

I'm not sure what it is I can't do, but I'm certain in this moment whatever it is is impossible. I wait until the laughter fully recedes before I quickly clomp back home.

When I get there, I sneak in the front door.

Or, I try to, anyway.

I catch a glimpse of my father dropping his work bag on the kitchen counter. He must have heard the door click, because he looks up and locks eyes with me, dropping his keys on the floor as he does.

"What the...?"

I vanish up the stairs before I can hear the final word and nearly tumble into my room. I shut the door and lock it behind me, listening with dread as the pounding footsteps get closer.

15

———

I can hardly hear the volley of knocks as I walk into the open wall.

Thank god.

If I was trapped in my room for this patriarchal assault, I don't know what I would've done.

The door-hammering behind me dissipates, and the corridor gets darker. I turn to see the opening I had come through closing up like vines. All the better. My parents can break the door down and find nothing for all I care.

I clunk through the wallspace, following the dull glow to Violet's room.

The door is wide open, the television playing reruns of *Mayberry* softly. I step into the room and sink onto the vanity stool without even a look at Violet. I cup my hands over my face and slump onto the tabletop, knocking over a collection of makeup bottles with a clatter of clinks.

"I couldn't do it," I tell her. "I saw some kids from school and ran home."

Mayberry mumbles through the air lazily. Beneath the buzz, I think I hear the stomping of loafers far away.

Violet sighs. It's a sound that's two parts pity and two disappointment, though it's the latter that echoes in my ears.

"That sucks," I hear her say. She pauses a few beats before speaking again. "But hiding in here sucks even worse."

I know she's right. Even as I'm filling my cupped hands with tears, the comfort this place provided seems weaker.

Violet coughs, a racking sound that tells me she's gotten even sicker in the last hour.

"I don't want to tell them," I say. "I'm scared. You didn't see how angry my dad looked."

Violet's silence suggests she has no problem picturing it.

"What are you gonna do if you don't?" she asks finally, punctuating with a cough. "Pretend he never saw you? Live the rest of your life hiding away?"

The questions punch me in the gut. I cough into my hands, then raise my face from them. I look at Violet's reflection in the mirror, sniffing up as much snot as possible to regain a last shred of dignity.

I shake my head a second before saying, "No. No, I don't wanna do that either."

"You can't control how they react, but if you don't tell them, it just gets worse."

The cement hardening in my stomach tells me she's right. Even if my parents explode at me, at least they'll be exploding at the real me. I'll have nothing to hide anymore, and they'll have to accept it or not.

"Yeah."

We sit and listen to the conversations on the screen.

"So are you gonna do it?" Violet finally asks.

She coughs.

I work up the courage to respond for what feels like hours. My eyes focus on anything but what the mirror shows me. My painted face, Violet's concerned expression. I read the labels of every bottle on the vanity. *Matte Finish. Raspberry Red. 24-Hour Long-Wear Mascara.* For too long, these things have been my secret friends, vials I hide like an alcoholic hides liquor.

"Yeah," I say. "Yeah, I am."

"Then you better fix that makeup, girl."

I giggle and finally face the reflection in the mirror.

I'm shocked to find only one face looking back at me. But as I look closer, I see Violet's features in my own skin. I see her deep brown eyes, her oval jaw. I see a flutter of lashes accenting each eye, the dark shadow stolen from a riot grrrl zine. I see the streaks of mascara running down her cheeks, the only sign that she was just crying.

I see Violet.

I see me.

❧

WHEN I FIX MY MASCARA, I stand up and walk out of the room and down the hall. I expected to feel like a lamb led to slaughter, but instead I feel giddy, like I'm walking into the world for the first time. I can't wait to see my room, to see the trees out the window, through my own painted eyes.

As I reach the end of the corridor, the wall yawns open in front of me. Framed in it are my parents, sitting on my bed, staring stoically at the floor. My father looks frustrated, and my mom looks like a pipe ready to burst. They're only scared animals, and the fear that I felt moments ago flits away.

I pause at the opening.

This is it, I tell myself. *After this you can't go back.*

They haven't noticed me yet. I could turn and run, but my legs are spent and my heart is tired. It's time to face the facts.

I step into my bedroom, and my parents look at me wordlessly.

"I'm Violet," I tell them. "I'm a girl."

I expect my father to combust, remembering the hammering fist against my door earlier, but he stares silently, his thoughts only shapes under the surface of his skin. I can feel him studying every inch of me, from my painted features to the dress cut just below my knees. He doesn't seem to know what it all adds up to.

"What?" my mom asks. "What do you mean? You're Vernon."

Her explanation falls face-to-the-floor in between us. This isn't a matter of lapsed memory. I haven't forgotten who I am. I've remembered.

"I think you know what I mean, Mom."

She shifts.

"Is this why?" she asks, before faltering.

I know what she's asking, but I'm not sure I have the answer.

"Not exactly," I tell her. "The cutting was, I don't know. It felt like there was something under my skin trying to get out. Something I couldn't see unless I dug it out. The pain was, I dunno. Clarifying. But I figured it out now. I don't need that anymore."

A whisper of relief washes over her face, followed by more concern. She scrunches her brow.

"You figured out you were..."

"Trans, Mom. I'm a transgender girl."

"You figured...that...out by...cutting?"

We're speaking different languages, it seems. Struggling to translate each syllable.

"No," I sigh. "It wasn't the cutting, it was. I don't know. It was just time for me to figure this out, this feeling of displacement I've always felt. It wasn't the cutting. It was just me, thinking." I think of Violet, the space in the walls, everything I can never explain. "I was exploring. New parts of myself."

"Ah," she says.

My father's jaw is wound tight with wire.

"I went to a group," I tell them. "Like a church group, but for kids like me."

"No church group lets boys wear dresses," my dad spurts.

It hurts, but not as much as I expected it to.

"Just listen to him, honey," my mother says.

"Listen to *her*."

"What?"

"My pronouns are she/her," I tell them, though I could describing a Renaissance painting in Icelandic.

"Just listen to...your child," my mother says.

We have a lot of work to do.

The thought haunts me, but only in the way of a happy memory. This was the hard part. And now, it's nearly over. I've put it as plain as I can, and it's up to them to keep up if they want.

"It's called *Gay All Day,* and it's a group of queer and trans kids in town. They're really nice, and I've already make some friends there."

Having born witness to my long-suffering solitude, my mother seems a little taken aback by my use of the word *friends.*

"Well, that's," she says. "That's really good."

My father squints at the ground.

"So this means you want to wear dresses?" he asks.

"Sometimes," I say. "But not always. I like jeans, too."

Something in the answer doesn't satisfy him, but he doesn't argue. My mother rubs his back. I've never seen him so unsure, his foundation so shattered.

"And, Violet, that's the name you want?" my mom asks.

I nod. Hearing someone else say it makes me soar.

"I like the name Violet," I say. "It's my name."

"Okay," my mother says. She stands up. "Me and your father are going to go talk. You're going to need to give us time with this. But remember we love you."

She gestures for my dad to get up, and he does. She shoots him a look.

"We love you," he says.

Words my father says rarely, but when he does he means it.

"Okay," I say. "I love you, too."

My mom smiles sadly at me and guides my father out of the room. The door clicks shut behind them, and I hear them shuffle into their own bedroom. With another click, I'm alone.

I sit down on my bed, stunned by what has just taken place. I'd built this up for so long that in comparison the reality seems laughable. I laugh at it. Then I laugh at my parents, and I laugh at myself. I laugh at the wall where I had first discovered the girl named Violet, and I laugh because it doesn't have to exist anymore. I laugh because I'm laughing, and I laugh because I'm laughing at my own laughter.

I look through the window at the breezing trees outside, and I laugh at them.

I see my reflection in the glass, the face of Violet, the face of a girl, and I laugh at it. Laugh at me, Violet, the girl.

My name is Violet, and I am a girl.

ACKNOWLEDGMENTS

Thank you to Christoph, Leza, and CLASH, who believed in my idea from the beginning. Thank you to Alix, my partner, whose love, ideas, and support keep me afloat. Thank you to the queer and trans community in my life and across the world who continually inspire to me to create and fight and breathe as my true self.

And thank you to the many writers and readers who I have met along the way, and who have supported who I am and what I do.

This is for all of you.

ABOUT THE AUTHOR

Katy is a queer transwoman who writes strange and senti-
mental horror-adjacent fiction. Her first novella, *Winnie*, was
published by Eraserhead Press in 2018, and her stories can be
found in *Lazermall* by Filthy Loot and *The New Flesh* by Weird-
punk Books, among other collections. She currently inhabits
the forests of the Pacific Northwest with her partner and their
three catchildren.

Follow her on Instagram @kittymyshellqueen

ALSO BY CLASH BOOKS

DARRYL

Jackie Ess

MARGINALIA

Juno Morrow

BORN TO BE PUBLIC

Greg Mania

LIFE OF THE PARTY

Tea Hacic

GIRL LIKE A BOMB

Autumn Christian

HEXIS

Charlene Elsby

CENOTE CITY

Monique Quintana

I'M FROM NOWHERE

Lindsay Lerman

THE HAUNTING OF THE PARANORMAL ROMANCE AWARDS

Christoph Paul & Mandy De Sandra

WE PUT THE LIT IN LITERARY

clashbooks.com

FOLLOW US

Twitter

IG

FB

@clashbooks

EMAIL

clashmediabooks@gmail.com

PUBLICITY

Lindsey Ferris

clashbookspublicity@gmail.com

www.ingramcontent.com/pod-product-compliance
Lightning Source LLC
Chambersburg PA
CBHW021735190726
48288CB00009B/3053